Shanghai – A Year to Remember

Vijay Menon

COPYRIGHT NOTICE

© 2018 Vijay Menon. All rights reserved. This book or parts thereof may not be reproduced in any form, stored in any retrieval system, or transmitted in any form by any means – electronic, mechanical, photocopy, recording, or otherwise – without prior written permission of the author and publisher. For permission requests, please see the contact details below.

- Vijay Govind aka Vijay Menon – vm.in@gmx.com

For information about special discounts available for bulk purchases, sales promotions, fund-raising and educational needs, please contact Vijay Menon at vm.in@gmx.com

First Edition

ISBN-13: 978 19830 59759 (Amazon Only)

TABLE OF CONTENTS

Copyright Notice i

Foreword, Disclaimer, Whatever v

A Dedication vii

Remembering Our Inspiration ix

Part 1 – A Helping Hand 1

    Chapter 1.   A Chance Encounter 3

    Chapter 2.   Back-Breaking Help 8

    Chapter 3.   The Train Ride 12

    Chapter 4.   Talking About Life 15

    Chapter 5.   The Incident 21

    Chapter 6.   Heading Back Home 24

    Chapter 7.   She Lives on the 13th Floor 27

    Chapter 8.   The Grass is Greener 36

    Chapter 9.   Heading Back Home 41

Part 2 – Wise Men Say 45

    Chapter 10.   The Cure for A Hangover 47

    Chapter 11.   So Jaded 54

    Chapter 12.   Sparks in Xintiandi 58

    Chapter 13.   The Tango 73

    Chapter 14.   Penny for Your Thoughts 81

    Chapter 15.   Making Pancakes Her Way 85

    Chapter 16.   One More Request 90

    Chapter 17.   An Evening's Worth of Text Messages 96

    Chapter 18.   Something Like A Dinner Date 105

Part 3 – All Good Things 123

    Chapter 19. Fast Forward and Rewind 125

    Chapter 20. The Day After the Dinner Date 134

    Chapter 21. The Long Walk 142

    Chapter 22. A Long Text Message 147

    Chapter 23. While Waiting for A Response 151

    Chapter 24. Different Stages of Heartbreak 164

    Chapter 25. Insanity Comes Calling 175

    Chapter 26. Carpe Diem 184

Epilouge 189

FOREWORD, DISCLAIMER, WHATEVER

Disclaimer: This is a work of fiction. Names, characters, places, and incidents either are the products of the author's imagination or are used in the fictitious context. Any resemblance to actual persons, living or dead, businesses, companies, events, or locales is entirely coincidental.

Okay, that's out of the way, lets to the real point.

As one can expect, a fiction like this is usually a work inspired by our accumulated experiences with a bit of imagination thrown in, and it would be unfair to claim that this work is entirely imaginary. I have made a sincere effort to ensure the identity of people from real life, whom I may or may not have slipped into this story, is sufficiently masked. What I am really trying to say is, if you think I am writing about you, please pause for a minute to ask yourself, how unique your life really is. We all are in a rat race and the way we behave is influenced to some extent by the people we are forced to interact with, day in day out. As motivational speaker Jim Rohn aptly said, "We are the average of the five people we spend the most time with."

The story narration is in the first person due to the ease of writing this story. I lead a normal, boring and uneventful life, more or less, happy with whatever I have in my life.

Similarly, I am not the most creative person when it comes to names (amongst many other things), and so, if you see your name, trust me it is not you. Sometimes, I am so happy that I am not yet a parent as I would give my daughter or son, one of the most generic names in the world. I am that lazy.

The story is set in Shanghai, a city I have called home for close to ten years now but can easily take place in any large city where millions of people live in close proximity to each other but couldn't be more alone. It is only in such places you will see a long sequence of unbelievable coincidences happening to a normal guy. Thus, the city is irrelevant, only the characters in this story are relevant, but that is for you to decide.

Following the same spirit, I have tried to get rid of ethnic biases in this story. The characters can be from any nation, or any ethnicity, but me being an Indian at heart and in spirit, and me having lived in China for so long, might have influenced the tone of the story.

I struggled with the idea of a pen name for a long time as my motivation to write this story was very different. I was trying to write for someone else, and for money, whereas I should have been writing for myself and for the joy of it. And, yes, I feared failure and needed a name to hide behind in case this book tanked. For now, I am willing to see how far this name goes.

The book APE by Guy Kawasaki and Shawn Welch inspired me to write a self-published book. I have been trying to publish something since forever; I didn't lack ideas, I lacked the motivation and I got lazy as time passed.

English is not my first language, so all the deficiencies you will see in language, especially around the grammar usage, is entirely mine. Giving the limitation in my vocabulary, you will see that I have repeated many words. If you wonder why all my characters speak bad Indian-English, the aforementioned reasons hold.

I would have loved to write this in Mandarin Chinese, but I am not there yet. My Chinese teachers will die of a heart attack and then come back as a zombie to kill me if I even attempted to write this book in Mandarin Chinese.

Dear family members, thank you for wanting to read whatever I wrote, but don't read after this point. I love you all very much, and I don't want you all to hate me. This book is nothing like my blog.

My apologies in advance to all the Indians, the Chinese, and the Italians. I am not really that culturally inclined. Also, my apologies to the people in the medical profession, I didn't bother doing any sort of research into how the human body works.

I have not plagiarized anyone's work, and that possibly shows in the overall (lack of) quality in the book.

A DEDICATION

For My Family,

    You and I, we been through ups and downs.

For My Friends,

    You and I, we celebrated life together.

For My Past Loves,

    You and I, we survived and endured each other.

For My Shanghai,

    You and I, we did have some good times.

For My Bengaluru,

    You and I, we can never be apart.

For My Gina,

    You and I, our story is yet to be written.

REMEMBERING OUR INSPIRATION

My Dear Amma (Mother), you would have loved this book, at least tolerate it, even if the whole world hated it. Thank you for being my mother and thank you for your constant motivation.

Rajalakshmi Shivdas (Nair)

Daughter, Sister, Wife, Mother, Aunt, and Fabulous Chef

She welcomed people with a warm smile, an open heart and some of the best Indian foods ever. We will miss you

30th May 1956 – 10th Feb 2018

PART 1 – A HELPING HAND

Chapter 1.   A Chance Encounter

It was just a few minutes after half-past-six in the morning and I, Anandapadmanabhan Nair, was on my way to the Shanghai metro line 2 stop of *Loushanguan* Road. I am guessing here, but I think, my parents couldn't find a longer name that went well with the surname "Nair" – I went by Anand. It was February, a week before Chinese New Year holidays, and the weather was cold and air crisp. It was a Saturday morning.

I was exhausted and elevated at the same time. I had this silly grin plastered on my face as I stumbled towards the metro station. I have been hanging out with some of my best friends in Shanghai since the previous night. The holiday season was just around the corner and it was time to catch up with my friends in Shanghai, or whoever stayed back. As is the case with the holiday season in China, there was a lot of drinking and smoking, followed by a lot of singing, more drinking and more smoking at the KTV – a place where talentless people like me go to sing. I wanted to hang out some more time with my friends, but common sense prevailed, as there was no way I could stay awake and no way I could drink anymore.

At around 3 AM, I dragged Allen Huang, my closest friend in Shanghai, into a taxi outside the KTV and took him back to his house. Thankfully his wife, Jean Li who was also my close friend, was not at home; she had gone back to Hangzhou with her parents for Chinese New Year celebrations. Allen had negotiated a dicey truce with his folks who are hard-core Shanghainese (*like five generations in Shanghai, ignore Pudong's existence kind of Shanghainese – Pudong is newer, and in some cases fancier part of Shanghai*), and his wife and in-laws, who were all new Shanghainese, but in their hearts hard-core Hangzhouers (*Like sing praises for the West Lake and all of its history kind of Hangzhouers*). Based on the truce, he will spend the Chinese New Year's Eve with his parents and Chinese New Year with his wife and in-laws.

I didn't envy Allen one bit.

I tried getting a ride using one of those ride-hailing platforms, but at that time of the night, I was having no luck finding any ride. I should have asked the taxi that dropped us to wait for me. Traditional taxi guys were not up during that time or didn't want to deal with a foreigner at that time and, despite adding RMB 10 tip in a country where you don't generally tip (Perhaps that was the problem – that I added too small a tip). In short, I couldn't hail a ride or find a taxi. The Metroman app on my phone told me that if I waited till 5:46 AM, I can get the first train passing through the Line 2 metro station there. That was just a couple of hours away. As Allen was fast asleep, I decided to make myself at home. I went to his kitchen made a cup of instant coffee, then raided Allen's bar for some Bailey's Irish cream and added a generous splash into my coffee.

I quietly sat down on Allen's plush couch in his living room and started enjoying my coffee. I opened my kindle app and selected a book to re-read... Day of the Jackal looked good. I have a simple principle – when drunk, don't strain the brain too much. Rereading a well-read book is the least stressful activity in the world for me. I started reading the book and eventually finished the coffee.

I could hear Allen mumbling in Shanghainese, which is the local Shanghai dialect, in his sleep. I made one more coffee with Irish Cream to help pass the second half of two hours, the only problem being that I finished the second one in under five minutes. The second coffee was a little stiffer than the first one and, soon started nodding off.

I am not sure when I slipped into a sleep, but I snapped awake at around quarter past six. Allen would be okay for me to stay over until I sobered up, but I decided I better head back home... I sleep-talk in English and don't want Allen to hear some of my rants. I got out of the couch, which was really hard when you are drunk and the couch is super plush. I made it out of the couch and tip-toed to the toilet to relieve myself. I then splashed some cold water on my face to wake me up completely.

I left the coffee mug in the sink; I knew Allen has an *A'yi* who comes in every day to clean up. I quietly slipped out of the apartment and sent Allen a tongue in cheek message thanking him for his "hospitality" as I rode the lift down to the first floor.

I was fairly familiar with the area but given my general lack of sense of direction and my current state, I decided to take help of *GaoDe* maps. I open the app, typed out the metro station name in Chinese, and after a bit of confusion around which direction is which, started stumbling towards the metro station. I could feel the onset of a mild hangover, and all the morning noises were starting to irritate me. I took out my earphone from my pocket, untangled the wires, plugged it to my iPhone and started playing some songs I recently discovered on QQ Music. I sang along for a while but ended up scaring some old lady and her dog on their morning walk. These people can never appreciate the primal magic in my voice. In any case, I stopped singing as my throat was really sore. I popped a piece of chewing gum into my mouth and light a cigarette. I inhaled deep and felt the sweet suffocating hold of nicotine-tar cloud grip my lungs and felt the mist in my head clear away slowly.

The walk to the metro stop took me twenty minutes. The walk and the crisp Shanghai air helped clear my head a bit more and kept me awake. I crushed out the cigarette, entered the metro station and walked down to the metro entrance.

Usually, in Shanghai, if you have a large enough bag like the laptop backpack one would carry to the office, you are required to pass it through the X-ray scanner before you enter the metro station. Since it was really early, for a weekend, and since the guards were barely awake, they didn't insist on checking everyone and were ignoring pretty much anyone entering the station, including me. Maybe the number of people travelling at that point is so less that they figured that not much of a damage can be done, in case someone wanted to carry any "dangerous article".

As I approached the entrance gate, I noticed a girl with a stunning figure struggling with a large bag at the entrance. I have to be honest; I noticed her shapely figure way before I noticed what she was doing. She was trying to get the bag into the station after swiping the metro card. As I approached the entrance, I couldn't help but admire. She was dressed in a simple but elegant black dress which flowed gracefully over the curves of her body. I am a guy and I can't describe this any better, but I can tell you, in my humble opinion, what she was wearing was nothing really fancy.

As I got closer to her, I caught a whiff of her perfume which accentuated her whole presence. Quite suddenly, all my weariness was forgotten and rest of the mist in my head cleared out.

The girl barely glanced at my direction, as I approached the gate, but then that was not abnormal. I deserved a second look only when there was snot dripping out of my nose. She was focussed on getting the bag inside the metro station. The guards at the scanner didn't bother to help her and stood there admiring the view, and I must admit, it WAS some view.

I made up my mind that I must at least offer my help.

I gently tapped the lady on her shoulder and asked, "Excuse me miss, do you need some help with the bag?"

The lady turned around with a shocked and confused expression on her face, which deepened after seeing my face. And what a face it was! I have seldom seen a more attractive face in Shanghai. She had a near perfect face, with full lips which were partially open in surprise, a surprisingly perfect nose, shining straight hair that framed a beautiful oval face, sharp sparkling black eyes (none of those iris enhancement contacts) and near flawless skin even without any make-up, as far as I can see. She was about four inches shorter than me and had a slender, graceful figure.

By the expression on her face, I assumed that she didn't understand me. I was worried that this would be one of those awkward situations, wherein I would make a jackass of myself due to the fact that English is not a common language in Shanghai or China. I had taken the chance as Shanghai is better off when it comes to English when compared to some other places in China. The fact that I was drunk *Malayalee* trying to put on an American accent actually made things worse; Any person who understood normal English generally gets confused when I do my American accent, and this is when I am very sober. I decided to ask her once more before I made myself scarce.

"Do you...", I repeated, "need... some... help... with... the bag?" enunciating as clearly as possible and pausing after each phrase, this time in a serious British Accent, which usually makes things worse when combined with my *Malayalee* accent (which by the way, is a subject of much ridicule, even in India). To leave no room for doubt, I mimed each of the actions while talking. There! That should drive home the message, wherever she's from and whatever language she may speak. I was thinking up the words in Chinese for a last-ditch attempt in case the British accent failed as well.

She studied my face for some time and stared into my eyes for about ten seconds. I think she was trying to gauge what sort of a person I was. Shanghai, like any other big city, is not the kind of place where a random person would offer help to another random person without expecting something in return. Trust is a currency that was rare in this part of the world.

"Uh... Yes... Sure, I could do with some help. Thank you", she said partially recovering from the shock of some random dishevelled Indian offering help.

If you find that unbelievable, let me tell you right away, that I was really surprised when she accepted my offer. I was already mentally prepared to hear "No thanks" and my whole body was ready to shrug off the rejection and go back home. By the way, her English was perfect, with a slight Australian lilt to it. I had to admit her English sounded way better than mine.

I flexed my muscles, sucked in my gut, bent my knees and hoisted the bag on to my left shoulder.

Chapter 2.   Back-Breaking Help

The bag she was wrestling with was one of those large ugly bags designed fit a large folding bike and it objectively weighed a ton, like it had a dead body in it. I had some difficulty in lifting that bag, leave alone move it. I am no weakling, but I had to strain my muscles greatly to make it look somewhat effortless. Thankfully, she lent me a helping hand. I thought I would surely injure my back or dislocate my shoulder trying to lift and move the thing, but I managed to get it inside the station.

Damn, I needed to quit smoking (*again*) and needed to start lifting weights (*again*).

She observed my efforts while standing beside me and followed me into the station after the bag was inside. I could see that she looked a little worried as if it might be filled with stacks of cash.

I stepped on to the escalator and gently set down the bag behind me. The girl stepped on the escalator and behind the bag. I rubbed my shoulder and back to relieve the ache in my poor muscles. I couldn't help but wonder how the hell she got the bag to the X-ray machine, but my brain was tired and shrugged off that thought. I just wanted to get back home, take a long hot shower and sleep off all the weariness. I heaved the bag off the escalator just as we reached landing at the bottom and stumbled to the nearest seats.

I carefully placed the bag on to the platform and sat down on the seats. I had never truly appreciated these cold metals seats as they somehow reminded me of hospitals. That moment, I was grateful for these seats. The girl sat next to me, opened her handbag, put her metro card in and took out her cell phone. She fiddled with it for a while, and put it back into her handbag, while I rubbed my poor aching shoulder.

"Which direction are you heading to?" I asked after she was done with her cell phone, still rubbing my shoulder.

"I am heading towards the Pudong side, Century Park to be exact", she said pointing to the left. "How about you? Which way are you heading to?" she asked.

"I am heading the same way", I said with the slight smile. "I live somewhere close to Century Park station as well."

Actually, I lived midway between the Science and Technology Museum station and Century Park station, but technically my apartment was right next to Century Park.

"Okay..." she replied, after a moment of hesitation. She appeared to be in thinking, and she turned to me a couple of times as if to ask something. She said nothing both the times. I guessed that she might want some help at the metro station as well but was too embarrassed to ask me.

"Do you need some help with the bag... I mean, to get it into a taxi and once we reach Century Park?" I volunteered, though I was not sure how far, I can carry that bag. She had no reason to trust me, so I was ready for a rejection.

Her face lit up and I knew what her answer would be even before she said, "Thank you, that's most kind of you". She pointed at the bag, "I don't think I can get this to the taxi alone."

Taxi is a nice idea, I thought. I can drop the girl back to the taxi stand, then head back to my little apartment in the same taxi, for a long hot shower and long sleep. As I made this plan, I glanced at my watch and realised that it was already few minutes after 7:00 AM. I have been awake for almost 24 hours. I stifled a yawn and rubbed my tired eyes. A glance at the metro TV conveyed the fact that we needed to wait for another 5 minutes or so before the next train arrived. Exactly the right time to introduce myself.

"I am Anandapadmanabhan Nair," I said with an awkward smile and added, "You can call me Anand."

"Ana... nda... mana... wha... Sorry?" She asked me with a slightly bewildered look on her face.

"Ah, Forget it. Just call me Anand. Everyone calls me that, that's much easier". I was quite familiar with the confusion most Chinese had with my name. Moreover, if I start correcting her ridiculous pronunciation, I will probably need more time than the one hour we spend on the train.

"OK, Anand it is then. It's nice to meet you, Anand. I guess from your long name, and the Indian accent, that you might be an Indian" she said, pronouncing my name as Ana-and. She paused for a couple of seconds and introduced herself, "I am *Zhang Hui*, you can call me Nicole".

"Nice to meet you, Nicole. Thai and Sri Lankan people have long names as well, but yes, I am an Indian. From the south of India", I responded. I burned a bit from the accent comment... Damn my *Malayalee* accent. I could feel the hesitation in even disclosing her name.

We had a minute more to go before the train arrived at the platform. I knew that I better drag the bag near the edge of the platform so that I wouldn't hurt myself by trying to board the train too fast with the bag. I took a deep breath and bent my knees a bit, yanked the bag off the platform, carefully carried the bag to the edge of the platform and placed it behind the yellow line. My right shoulder felt bruised from all that effort and I massaged my shoulder to ease the discomfort in my shoulder. I couldn't feel a whole lot of muscles at that point in time.

What the hell am I doing and why the hell am I doing this? I asked myself. I knew from my general experience that this, whatever "this" was, was not going to go anywhere. Maybe, I should just make some excuse, help her get the bag into the metro and take the next train. Nothing is ever going to happen to me, so I guess I have to be happy with this little encounter, walk away right now.

Grow a spine, grow a spine... just grow a fucking spine and don't let people use you. Tell her, you need to take the next train, I told myself, quite vehemently.

That thought evaporated when Nicole walked up to me, smiled at me, and said, "Thank you so much, Anand. I am really grateful. You were so kind to help me."

"Don't mention it, I think it's something people should do – help each other", I shrugged it off.

I guess it is true that some men do think with their genitals and not their brains, especially when it comes to dealing with women. Her mere presence had already put me off guard. When she walked up to me and stood so close to me, my throat constricted and I started feeling dizzy and confused... Or it might have been all that alcohol and cigarettes. I had a crazy imagination that had a tendency to run wild and would raise my hope unnecessarily, so I continued whipping myself mentally so that I don't get carried away by the mere fact that a (beautiful) girl accepted my help and smiled at me.

Chapter 3.   The Train Ride

As I was beating up myself in my head, the train arrived at the platform and Nicole tugged at my arm, indicating that we need to go. I guess I had a blank, brain-dead look on my face and she had to make sure that I have not become a zombie or something. I lifted the bag, with the now perfected technique of bend of knees and yank and boarded the train. Thankfully, the train was nearly empty. Nicole and I sat down on the nearest available seats, with the bag placed at our feet. We sat together, but I maintained a respectful distance as I was worried I will nod off and fall on her.

Nicole thanked me for my help again and before I could respond with a self-deprecating comment, she got a call. She excused herself and took the call, as the train started moving. She started talking in Chinese and from my experience living in Shanghai, I knew this was going to be one of those long calls. I believe one can estimate how long a call is going to be by estimating the length and tone of the first "Hey" or "Hello". This was a long, high pitched equivalent of "Heeeeeeey" (or "*Weeeeeei*" in Chinese), that was about four seconds long.

Good time to check my phone.

I pulled out my phone and saw that there I had got a few messages. I started checking and responding to my text messages on WeChat (Chinese WhatsApp / Line equivalent) and WhatsApp.

As I read and replied to the messages, I started thinking what could be there in the bag, after all, Nicole was extra protective about the bag. She was busy chattering (quite expressively) on phone and for all practical purposes, I had ceased to exist. She seemed like a normal Chinese girl but, I was slightly paranoid and I was more than a little worried about what could be there in the bag. What if she's got a dead body inside? Have I unwittingly become an accessory to some crime? It certainly felt heavy enough to be a small dead body – I guess I have seen too many urban legend movies. This lady looked normal, was polite and friendly, but I value my life more.

I glanced at Nicole though the corner of my eyes and she was talking animatedly to her friend, *"Mmnhnnh Aaha Mmnhnnh Aaha, hao hao dui dui dui dui, zhidaole ya, Ha ha ha ha... Aiya! xiao si wo le!* (Mmnhnnh Aaha Mmnhnnh Aaha, good good yes yes yes yes, I know, Ha ha ha ha... OMG! that's so funny!)" If you lived in China, you know what I mean, and you know I'm not making this up.

She was completely oblivious to my presence and I decided that now is the right time to try and figure out what's inside the bag. I stretched my left leg and started furtively poking the bag with the tip of my shoes. Whatever was inside the bag felt hard like blocks of wood and it did not feel like a dead body (soft and squishy, I think). I quietly breathed a sigh of relief went back to my texts. Nicole was laughing again, possibly at some joke made by her friend.

One of the things that amazed me is the fact that the phone signal in the metro is quite good when you don't need it, like for making useless calls, gossiping on WeChat or WhatsApp or for browsing Weibo (Chinese twitter) and signal is really bad when you need it most, like when you have to make an urgent call or send an email to your boss or client.

As expected, since there was nothing urgent, I had a full signal and my internet was working perfectly. It's only when you have urgent stuff to do that your internet will stop working or you will run out of battery. I unlocked my phone and saw fifty-odd messages in my MBA groups and office group. Before I checked all those messages, I connected to the metro Wi-Fi, because I had been data bingeing this whole month and didn't have much data left. After connecting to the free Wi-Fi, I noticed that there was also a couple of personal messages from Allen. He was super happy to see me after a long time and wanted to know if I am still single. He wanted to introduce me to some of his wife's friends.

I knew most of Allen's wife's friends, and none of them ever wanted to meet me three years back, so this was very confusing for me. Perhaps they are all past their thirties now and willing to consider me as an option. Perhaps it's my "fancy" education in a so-called rich man's MBA School in Shanghai. This had happened more frequently, especially in the past couple of years. As far as I know, nothing has changed in my life in this time period, except finding a girlfriend around a year back and breaking up with her six months later. As I pondered over the mysteries of life in Shanghai and how the tables have turned, we arrived at People Square Metro Station – the busiest metro interchange in Shanghai and possibly in China.

As soon as the door opened, people dashed into the metro car and dived into available seats around us. This is something that never ceases to amaze me in China – the way people dash into the metro, look around maniacally, and dive into empty seats like their life depended on it. It doesn't matter how old or young you are, what profession you belong to, or what socio-economic strata you belong, you see this behaviour all throughout China. Let me assure you this is not the crazy violent rush you see in India as people board buses or the general compartment in trains with people pulling and dragging each other like crabs in a pot, but more like an organised chaos system with no hard feelings or emotions, in most cases. Interestingly actual fights broke over where people got to stand.

Anyhow, I digress. By the time the train started from people square, Nicole and I were squeezed together by people who had dived into space on either side. Nicole dragged the bag closer to her and placed a hand on the bag and continued to chatter with her friend. Her presence was starting to affect me again and I was conscious of tiniest of things I would have normally ignored like her soft shoulders brushing against my shoulders and sides of her thigh pressing against my thigh. I squirmed in the seat and moved away from her hoping that she wouldn't notice my movements. Unfortunately, her call ended at that exact moment and she noticed my movements.

Chapter 4. Talking About Life

Nicole turned her attention to me and mumbled an apology. I told her it is okay (and almost added, "I'm used to it") and since I couldn't think of anything else, asked her if she was from Shanghai or some other part of China.

She told me she was a new Shanghainese before and that her family was originally from some small city in Zhejiang. Her family had moved to Shanghai when she was six. She had lived in Shanghai until she finished her high school and migrated to Australia for her undergrad and post-grad studies. She worked in Sydney and Australia for about five years before coming back to Shanghai about four years back, as an Australian citizen. Although I was nodding my head and was trying the listen, my brain was furiously trying to estimate Nicole's age; math was never my strong point and adding up all those numbers gave me an aneurysm, but I reached a guestimate of 32-35. And... I also understood the reason behind her Aussie-like accent.

She told me that she was currently running her own business – one of those professional services that helped Chinese students prepare for undergraduate and graduate school applications to universities in US, UK, Canada Europe and Australia. She got the idea during her studies in Australia and saw that there was an opportunity for her in this segment, as she had a background in education services and there was a lot of demand from Mainland China for a western education (she was part of recruitment and admissions team for Melbourne University). In just under two years, she had grown her business to a premier educational services company with a solid revenue stream.

She then started questioning me about my life and work in Shanghai. I tried to engage her in a conversation, which seemed easier than normal. I told her I have been in Shanghai for more than nine years and I talked a bit about my education in Shanghai. She seemed genuinely surprised and asked more about my MBA. I downplayed it as much as possible as I barely passed and had struggled a bit to find my current job (wherein I had gone back to being an IT guy). I told her that I am just living up to the stereotype of Indians being in IT and told as little as possible about the company I worked for and my job, which was objectively not very interesting. I spoke about how I loved to travel around China and talked about some of the places I loved, like Huangshan or the Yellow Mountain. I was surprised to find that she had never been to Huangshan. This another thing that never ceased to surprise me – the fact that a lot of Chinese know about famous places, but they themselves have not gone to those places. I guess familiarity does breed complacency.

She was curious as to how I ended up in Shanghai, especially since most Indians she had come across wanted to immigrate to the US, UK or Australia/NZ. In a previous trip to Yiwu, she had seen a lot of Indian traders there, but she assumed that there are relatively few Indian professionals in Shanghai.

I told Nicole, how nine years back I was given an opportunity to go to either Australia or to Shanghai. Naturally, I had opted for Shanghai as work experience in China would look good on my resume. Also, the growth in China also meant better growth opportunities for me in the future.

Of course, I didn't disclose the fact that I was supposed to stay in Shanghai for only a year and then move to Melbourne on a more permanent basis, or that I stayed back in Shanghai initially because the world was in the sub-prime crisis and then for the sake of a girlfriend. In any case, at least on the paper, I had a good reason for staying back. I also informed her politely that she needs to update her knowledge base about Indians as there are a bunch of Indian professionals and business owners living in Shanghai. As far as I know, the numbers were in high thousands.

Sometimes, people ask the right question at the right time, that freaks the crap out of you. That's exactly what happened at that instant.

"But more than nine years?" she asked, her eyes searching my face inquisitively, "you must have had a really good reason for staying back" she concluded, sort of knowingly.

I blushed a bit and my ears burned at being caught. I recovered quickly and explained how I got promoted quickly in my company as I had helped build the relationship to three times the size in just two years. I wouldn't be able to do that in any western market given the market dynamics. This answer sort of pacified her, and she nodded in agreement.

She asked me if I am living with my family in Shanghai and I informed her that I was not married. She seemed surprised that I was not married and she said so, as her understanding was that all Indian men and women got married off by the age of 28 and 23 respectively by their parents, relatives and friends through "forced arranged marriages".

I was surprised that she knew even that much about Indian culture. To the average Chinese, India was the place where *Yindu Shen You* came from (An aphrodisiac oil that was supposedly made by Indian sages for erectile dysfunction, but most Indians have never heard of it) and the place where people have only curry to eat, that too with hand.

I told her things are changing fast in India, especially in the cities. I asked her how she knew so much about Indian culture, although it was inaccurate. She remarked that she used to interact a lot with Indians while in Australia, as there were a large group of Indian students in her university.

Before she asked any more questions, I put the ball back into her court.

"So, tell me, what's there in the bag? You seemed a little concerned, when I was handling it and why take the metro at all?" I asked her directly, rubbing my shoulder for emphasis. My brain was too tired to do the diplomacy thing.

She laughed and explained how she had taken an early train from Century Park to *Loushanguan* road to meet her vendor, as she didn't want to get caught in the *Hongqiao* Airport traffic. She had met the vendor at the metro station and had collected 100 copies of English test preparatory materials that her company had developed. To beat the traffic from Puxi to Pudong, she took the metro back to Century Park. It had taken her "forever" to get the bag into the metro station. I admired her commitment to saving money for her business, as I would have taken a taxi back home/office.

She was planning to mail these to students around Shanghai, as well as various cities around Jiangsu and Zhejiang, over the holidays. She ran the business from her apartment and also had an office located near the Shanghai Jiaotong University. As the Chinese New Year was approaching, she wanted to use the slack time to promote her business and clear the backlog. The fact that she did all this alone was a sign that she was possibly single, else there would be some other guy doing all this for her. Maybe her boyfriend was lying hungover at home or something, after all, it was the weekend. I slapped myself mentally again to remind myself to stop imagining things.

Despite the frequent reality check and mental slaps, I couldn't help but reflect on what just happened. I mean, I never get lucky when it comes to women. I have travelled alone in trains & flights since my early teens and never, not once, I have travelled with an attractive girl. I guess it's all a matter of statistics and probability in the long run. The law of averages must be catching up.

She was far too attractive and far too friendly for my comfort. As far as I know, I am neither very interesting nor the kind of person who rarely deserves a second glance. I was average in every possible way. For people who knew about the bell curve, I am the line that divided the curve into two – Extremely average. Strangely, she seemed to be genuinely interested in what I had to say and she listened to me with a smile on her face. It's perhaps that my accent was hard to understand and funny to the listener… Or she was genuinely a nice person.

This went on long enough to the point that I actually started considering the possibility that she might be crazy. My accent is funny, but not that funny. I pushed that thought out of my mind as well. As far as I can see, she didn't look crazy, so she was not talking to me because she has lost her mind.

I also noticed that she didn't have any ring on her finger increasing the possibility that she is probably not committed or she didn't show that she was committed or she didn't need a ring to show her commitment. I couldn't believe that such an attractive girl would be single and concluded that she cannot be single.

Stop thinking, I screamed at myself to just to stop this chain of thoughts.

I was finding it really hard to focus on what was going on in my current state. My overactive imagination did little to help me concentrate on what she was saying. After a while, the only thing that mattered to me was that she had a nice, soothing voice, and a gentle, polite manner.

My mouth felt cotton dry and there was this weird taste in my mouth from all that smoking and drinking. I desperately needed a smoke and needed a large cup of Starbucks latte. I popped another piece of gum into my mouth and chewed on it in an attempt to sweep away the rising grogginess and the weird taste in my mouth.

Nicole was following my actions, "You know what Anand? You look like you could use a large cup of coffee."

"Yes, I NEED a cup of coffee", I replied emphasizing on the word 'NEED', "and a cigarette. As soon as we get your bag situation sorted out. I will get a Grande triple shot Latte and smoke a couple of cigarettes."

I was hoping that she would cut in and say something like – No Anand, let me buy you a cup of coffee. This is the least I can do… for all your help.

I guess it was too much to hope for as Nicole just acknowledged my needs with a slight nod of the head and another smile. I sighed internally and accepted that I have a hyperactive imagination that needed some dialling back.

We had just started from Century Avenue metro station and the train had more or less emptied out as it was also an interchange station. Generally, few days before the Chinese New Year holidays there was going to be a lot of metro traffic, with people travelling to the airport and railway station, but at that point of time, the train was empty for Shanghai standards. I could see some air hostesses and airport staff heading, apparently in the direction of Pudong International Airport. Most of the commuters were dozing in their seats or was browsing or reading news on their smartphone. Metro TV was looping some funny videos knocked off from YouTube.

"What do you plan to do during the Chinese holidays? Will you be going back to India or travel around?" Nicole asked breaking into my chain of thoughts, random observations and general craziness.

"Well, I really hadn't planned anything worthwhile. Definitely not going home this time", I replied, "I will mostly stay back in Shanghai; I might go to Hangzhou or Suzhou for a day trip and I most definitely will do some metro surfing, as I plan to leave China by the end this year. I am hoping to meet some friends who are still in Shanghai, but mostly relax and surf the metro."

I have always known that there will reach a point in time where, I will have to move on from China and now that I have spent nine years here, I have started assuming that I will be heading back home "this year". Plus, I was tired of being alone.

"What do you mean by metro surfing?" she asked me as we pulled out of Shanghai Science and Technology Museum, "and, why are you leaving China?" Did I just detect a bit of disappointment in her voice or is it just my imagination? It has to be my imagination.

I knew that I had to drag the bag to the door as next stop was Century Park, so I excused myself and told her that we need to get ready to get out. I got up and dragged the bag right next to the door so that I can transfer to platform easily once I reach our stop. I rubbed my aching muscles, stretched my back and leaned against the safety railing or the safety bar for balance.

Chapter 5.   The Incident

Nicole stood up, walked next to me and asked: "So, what is metro surfing?"

It was clear that she understood my hesitation in talking about whatever reason I had for wanting to leave, changed the subject with that question.

Just as I started explaining what metro surfing is, the train screeched to a violent halt and Nicole was thrown forward in the momentum. She let out a little scream of surprise as she lost her balance. I moved reflexively into her path and caught her in my left arm and grabbed the safety bar with my right hand at the same instant. It was one of those moments where you were driven by intuition rather than by training, and things work in your favour. God knows that my general hand to eye coordination is horrible.

She threw her arm around my torso and grabbed on to me tightly as I regained the balance for both of us and prepared my body for reverse momentum. The reverse momentum was equally violent and I could barely hold on to the bar and Nicole at the same time, despite the fact that she was as light as a feather.

The train was quiet for a few seconds as people regained their bearings. The air hostess's suitcase had rolled off and she was frantically chasing the suitcase. The dozing guy was wide awake and looked around in confusion. My left hand was still wrapped around Nicole's slender body. She held on to me tightly with both her arms and her face was cradled against my chest. We remained like that, despite the fact that it was actually safe for us to let go of each other.

I became conscious of three things at the same time – that her body was moulded against me with her head buried into my chest, that the train was not moving, and that some people were staring at me. I am generally very awkward around strangers. A relative stranger holding on to me with as if her life depended on it and people staring at us, really threw me off guard. I started palpitating and broke into a cold sweat.

I gently let go of Nicole, expecting her to do the same. She just held on tighter. I cannot remember a more awkward situation in my life and it was at this point I started thinking what I should do. I was not smart enough to come up with any possible course of action.

She continued to hold me as the train engineer announced something in Chinese. I hoped it was an apology as breaking like that was a crazy thing to do to a bunch of sleepy passengers. She didn't let me go as the train started to move again. She held on to me as the train as we pulled into the Century Park Metro Station. It was at that point, I noticed she was shaking. She ignored me as I tried to inform her that we have reached her station. She ignored the people who stepped around us and her bag and glared at us.

She held on to me as the door closed and the train pulled out of the station. I relaxed and wrapped both my hands around her. I stroked her shoulders gently and told her everything is okay, and she can let go of me now. I could feel her heart thumping really hard. This was completely crazy, as I couldn't understand what was going on. Don't get me wrong, I didn't have a single sexual thought in my head, and I was actually more worried about Nicole and the people who were staring at me.

I wish I could say that I was the hero who sprung to action and helped her but I didn't do anything other than hold her and tried to talk to her in what I thought was soothing manner. Sometimes, I am so awkward with women that it's nothing short of a miracle that I have had any relationships in the past.

In any case, by the time we had reached the *Zhangjiang* high-tech park metro station, Nicole had stopped shaking as well. As the train pulled into the station, she squeezed me harder, mumbled something, and finally let me go. I let her go as well at the same instant.

My mind was racing now, and I was certain that she's crazy and my brain screamed at me to get out of there as fast as possible.

"Sorry, let's get out here, please", said Nicole repeated in a shaky voice as she stepped away from me. Okay, so that's what she mumbled.

She straightened up, smiled weakly and turned to face the door, which slid open a couple of seconds later. I grabbed the bag and stepped out on to the platform. There was a couple of row of those hospital-like metal chairs about five paces to the right. I had almost forgotten that the bag was heavy but was quite sufficiently reminded of its weight as I limped to the chair and dumped the bag gently next to the chairs. Nicole followed me unsteadily and sat down on one of the steel chairs. I could see that there was a vending machine on the platform. I told Nicole to wait for me and that I was going to get her some water. She just nodded her head weakly. *What is wrong with her?* I thought as I walked to the vending machine

The vending machine had some bottled water, ion drinks and some Chinese tea products. I selected a bottle of water and a bottle of ion drink as I was not sure what Nicole's would prefer. I scanned the QR code for Alipay payment and waited for the authorization. I sneaked a peak to see Nicole was sitting hunched over and biting her nails; she appeared to be in deep thought. My phone vibrated a couple of seconds later as the payment was approved and the machine dropped two bottles into the draw slot. I picked them both up and headed back to the seats.

"What would you like to have, water or this ion drink?" I asked her holding up the stuff I had just bought. She quietly reached for the ion drink and took it from my hand. I sat next to her and opened a bottle of water and took a sip of the water. Nicole's hands were shaking quite badly and couldn't open the bottle. I set down my water bottle on the seat next to me and gently took the bottle from her hand. I twisted the cap open and handed the bottle back to Nicole, who mumbled a 'thanks' and started sipping the drink.

We sat there quietly and drank from our respective bottles as trains continue to pass in either direction. I finished the water and waited for Nicole to finish her drink.

My 8:00 AM weekend alarm started ringing and I killed it. Nicole didn't seem to notice it and continued sipping on her drink.

She finally finished the drink and sat there dazed, probably wondering what to do next. I gently took the bottle from Nicole's hand. She snapped out of the daze and smiled at me again. I discarded the empty bottles in the nearest trash can and came back to where Nicole was seated. She looked much more composed and relaxed.

She looked up at me, and said, "Let's go back".

Chapter 6.   Heading Back Home

I heaved the bag to the edge of the platform and we waited for the next train to arrive at the platform. As we waited for the train to arrive, we stole glances at each other and pretended to not notice each other. I am not sure why she did that, but I did it because (at least partially) I was trying to gauge if she was okay. I could feel the awkwardness between us that hung like the thick Shanghai smog around us and I was thinking about ways to defuse this awkwardness when our train arrived at the station.

I placed the bag next to right side of the door and stood by it while Nicole stood on the left side and held on to the safety bar next to her. Between us, the awkwardness still persisted and I was getting bored of it. I sort of understood, rather guessed that Nicole was shaken up badly by the incident. Personally, this was a minor incident, but I have already experienced a few things in life, so my bars were a little higher than some other people.

Maybe I should ask her about this... I turned to face her and found that she had the expression of a person deep in their thoughts and knew it was best not to bother her.

We reached the Century park station and I followed Nicole out of the train dragging bag behind me. I placed the bag on the platform to shift the bag on to my other shoulder. The effects of lack of sleep, the alcohol and the adrenaline rush... all that was catching up with me. I couldn't help but wonder why Nicole couldn't get one of those foldable trolleys for moving around. It does look ugly and unstylish, but it would have made my life easier. To make things worse, we were far away from the escalator, like 10 meters "far".

As I stood there wondering, *what next*, Nicole's voice brought me back to earth.

"Are you okay?" Nicole asked with a concerned look on her face, "You don't look so good, Anand."

"It's the adrenaline rush", I told her with a wry smile on my face... more like a bile rush, but that sounds so uncool. "I am okay. Let's get to that escalator and get out of here"

"You look a bit grey; do you want to sit down for some time?" Her concern was very obvious in her voice.

I was indeed feeling grey and perhaps a bit green, but I shook my head and said with a weak smile, "I am fine, let's go find that taxi."

This obvious lie earned me another smile and we walked to the escalator.

By the time we reached the escalator, I was ready to drop dead. I let Nicole go ahead and I stepped on to the escalator behind her and placed the bag on the step behind me. The instant I placed the bag on to the elevator step, everything went black for a second. I managed to grip the railing on time, and I guess Nicole didn't notice as she was looking straight ahead. We got off the escalator and headed to the exit. For some reason, I was super motivated and super energetic as I swiped out of the station and exited the station without switching the bag between the shoulders. I might have been driven by adrenalin, as I had nothing else left in me.

We got out of the station and I found that there was a long queue of taxis waiting for us, and I felt a surge of relief. After all, I don't have to wait for a taxi and I can head back home sooner.

"Nicole, do you want me to come along with you, to help to get this to your apartment?", I offered, as we approached the taxi queue. She would have been too polite to ask me anyways.

"If that wouldn't bother you too much, I could use your help", she replied. The way she said that I felt like I was some knight in shining armour. I guess I have an honest, trustable face. *Thank God I was not a psychopath.*

"Not at all, let's get that taxi now," said I, as I hailed the first taxi in the queue. The taxi driver was kind enough to pull out of the queue and stop right in front of us. Maybe, he saw how pale I was and how close I was to vomiting. He opened the luggage boot and I pushed the bag into the boot. I felt light headed and felt high as all sensation rushed back into my muscles. I adjusted the bag so that, the driver can close the boot.

Nicole got into the back seat and I got in the front. Nicole told the taxi driver where she's going to and I was surprised to find that she lived in the apartment community very close to mine. I told her that we are neighbours and I lived right behind her community.

She told me that, her parents had bought it for her when she came back to Shanghai. She seemed surprised that I lived in that community right behind the one she was staying in. I don't blame her as the area is really expensive and I just don't look like someone who belonged there. Moreover, I was really lucky to find a house within my limited budget.

I was actually more surprised that she was not surprised that I understood Mandarin Chinese.

"So, tell me Anand do you work somewhere close by?" she inquired as the taxi sped toward her community.

I confirmed that I worked in the *Lujiazui* area of *Pudong*. Satisfied with the answer, she turned back to her phone to attend to her messages. There were so many things that I wanted to ask her, starting with why she reacted the way she did on the train. I was tired beyond words, and Nicole was texting someone, so I started nodding off despite the fact that her apartment complex was less than a kilometre away.

Chapter 7.   She Lives on the 13th Floor

About five minutes later we reached the apartment block and I woke up with a start. I am not sure why, but I mumbled an apology and got out of the car. The driver got out to help take the bag out of the trunk. I wanted to help him as he was a frail looking guy and I was worried he might snap like a twig, but my worry was misplaced as the guy was as strong as an ox and hefted the bag out fairly easily. I steeled my core as he passed the bag on to my shoulder. I stood there for a second as my body got accustomed to the weight of the bag. My mid-section felt weird and I assumed that its six-packs forming on my abs due to all the strain.

I started walking slowly to the building as Nicole paid the taxi driver. As I reached the main door, some kind soul who was stepping out of the building held the door open for me, probably after seeing my face which was some shade of curry-green. I was sure I looked like I was about to vomit but took a couple of deep breaths and recovered. Nicole followed me into the building and I motioned her to lead the way.

Nicole turned left into the corridor and I followed her, she turned left again to get to the lift bay. Thankfully, the lift was already on the first floor and Nicole hit the 'up' arrow to open the lift.

"Anand, thank you. I am not sure how to thank you", she said with a smile on her face as the lift door opened and she got in. This is the characteristics of some of the Chinese I have come across, they thank people repeatedly for the same thing.

"That's okay. Let's get to the lift, the bag is a *bit* heavy", I told her with a wink, and smile on my face as I followed her into the lift and she let out a short laugh.

I got into the lift that Nicole had held open for me. Yes, I was totally ungentlemanly... She swiped her access card and pressed thirteen, which I found interesting as this was the same floor I lived on. I decided against dropping the bag on the floor (I couldn't stand the thought of lifting the bag again) and leaned against the mirrored walls of the lift. Nicole stood next to me, with a thoughtful look on her face. She was probably thinking, how best to get rid of me. It was almost funny for me and I would have laughed but that instant a wave of nausea hit me. I involuntarily groaned as I fought back the sensation.

Nicole was startled by the sound that emanated from me and turned to look at me. Her eyes became as big as a saucer when she saw my face.

"Oh, your face look green, are you fine?" she asked me, with a mix of concern and horror in her voice.

"I am fine, I just really need to use the washroom, after I keep this in your office. If you don't mind, may I use your washroom?" I told her as the lift stopped and dinged thirteen.

"Of course, you may use the washroom and... You don't have to keep the bag into the office" she asserted. I guess, she trusted me enough to allow me, a stranger, into her home, for however brief it might be. For all you know, I could be a serial killer or a rapist, but again thank God I am not. A thought suddenly hit me – she might be one of those psychopaths who get men into her home and castrates them for revenge.

I checked my thoughts, as I came to realize that this is what the society is done to us – no one trusts no one, and no one is willing to help anyone.

The lift dinged thirteen and the lift door opened silently. She stepped out of the lift and held the door open for me. I stepped out of the lift and followed her into the apartment. Thankfully her apartment was right next to the lift – literally, a hop, skip and jump away – not that I could hop, skip or jump with that massive bag on my shoulder. Nicole had opened the apartment door for me. I stepped into the apartment and with Nicole's help, placed the bag down into her dining area.

The effect was magical; I felt so light that I was certain that I would levitate. I stood there for a few seconds enjoying the sensation until nausea hit me again. *Yup, that one is not going to stay down.*

"May I use your washroom, please?" I asked Nicole calmly, after gulping down whatever was rising up my throat.

"Sure, the washroom is right behind you", she said. She took one look at me and added, "Let me get some water for you, you go ahead, okay?" She seemed genuinely concerned and I was honestly touched by this concern, even in my current state.

I walked into the bathroom as coolly as possible; what can I say? Ego can be a bitch.

I close the bathroom door and locked the door behind me. The bathroom was obsessively clean and smelled nice, the way it would for a single girl. It was all a pink blur. I knelt next to the toilet bowl, opened the lid and started vomiting into the bowl, as silently as possible.

I heaved out whatever was there in my stomach and after about five minutes, I was done. I stood up shakily, feeling slightly better and feeling a whole lot lighter. I wiped the edges of the bowl clean with a piece of toilet paper, flushed twice, and walked to the wash basin. Everything in the bathroom came to focus, it was nauseatingly pink and well organized. I rinsed out my mouth and washed my face in the washbasin. The ice-cold water felt really nice. I "borrowed" some of Nicole's Korean toothpaste which was, pink and berry flavoured. I brushed my teeth with my index finger and rinse out my mouth with a Korean mouthwash.

As I was gargling my mouth (as quietly as possible), I hear a gentle knock on the door followed by Nicole's concerned voice coming through the door, "Hey, you okay in there?"

I quickly and silently spat out the mouthwash, before responding, "I am fine, sorry... I will be out soon."

"Oh no, no, no", she replied quickly, "It's all right, please take your time."

I washed out my mouth one last time with the ice-cold water from the tap and splashed some more ice-cold water on my face, before getting out of the bathroom.

I felt like a new man at that point.

I walked out of the bathroom to find Nicole sitting on the couch in the living room. Now that my senses had cleared up and nothing else was competing for my attention, she looked even more attractive.

"Listen, I borrowed some of your toothpaste and mouthwash", I said with an awkward smile, and added, "I am going to head back home now."

"Hey, come on, that's okay. You look much better", she said with a smile that lit up the whole room, "I have ordered coffee for us – Two triple Grande lattes from Starbucks. I also ordered some food for us. I hope you are okay with coconut & hazelnut scones. Why don't you have that and then go back home?"

She got up from the couch as she was talking and handed me a bottle of water. *Damn, she was so nice! Or she was a total psychopath, who will castrate me after the coffee.* I slapped myself mentally and checked my thoughts.

I look around the living room and saw that place was tastefully and minimally decorated. Most furniture in the living room except the couches were made with sandblasted, tempered glass, and steel. The living room was well lit and opened out to a large balcony where she had kept her foldable bike. The largest wall in her living room, the wall opposite the sofa she was seated, was covered with a topographical map of the world. It was about two meters high and four meters wide. What was really interesting was that there were no borders on the map and it was shaped like a butterfly. A dozen or so photos of varying sizes were scattered on the map. It was clear that these were photos from the places she visited, and size of the photos perhaps denoted the importance to her. I could make out Nicole's smiling face in front the Taj Mahal, the Great Pyramids of Giza, Opera House in Sydney, her silhouette in front of Angkor Vat, three or four photos in Europe (I recognised Eiffel Tower and Charles bridge in Prague), and a scatter of photos from across the United States.

"It's a nice place you got here", I said while admiring the map, "You have decorated it really well. I like the idea of the map, I would probably steal this idea for my home in India."

She looked at me and for a moment I thought, I saw a flash of what I thought was sadness. Whatever the emotion was, she recovered fast.

"It's okay, I guess. My folks allowed me to decorate it whatever way I liked", she said casually, and she changed the subject abruptly and asked me "Do you live alone or with a roommate?"

"I live alone", I should have added 'now' to the end of that sentence, as my ex-girlfriend used to live with me on and off before my breakup about six months back, "It's more convenient that way" I added, trying to sound casual. She nodded, hopefully in agreement with me.

We both fell silent for a minute, not knowing what to say. At least I didn't know what to say and I soon discovered that she was thinking how to say what she wanted to say.

"Anand, I have been thinking", she said breaking the silence, "If you have time, may I invite you for a lunch or a dinner? I wanted to thank you properly for your kind help." She sounded hesitant as if she's not used to doing this and it did look like it took a lot of courage for her to ask.

I felt my jaw drop open, and I could see Nicole blush at my spontaneous reaction. This day was getting more and more unbelievable as it went by. Thankfully, before either of us could say anything more, her phone started ringing. She looked at me briefly before answering the call. I figured out from the conversation that it was someone from the coffee store. It sounded as if the delivery guy was already on his way and would be here in ten minutes or so. I had made up my mind and waited impatiently for the call to be done.

She disconnected the phone and we both started talking at the same time.

"I am happy…" I said and paused.

"I understand if…" she said and paused.

We stared at each other for about ten seconds; it felt as if we were both afraid of what the other had to say. I have no idea what she was thinking, but I knew that I had nothing to lose.

I manned up and blurted out, "Thank you for your invitation. I am okay for lunch or dinner… whenever you have time."

She seemed pleased with my response, and with her head tilted to the ceiling started thinking aloud, "Next week is Chinese New Year; I can finish the work this week. I am not travelling anywhere, so I'm free the whole of next week. Let's meet sometime next week. Can I have your cell number and WeChat ID?"

I gave her my number and showed her my WeChat QR code, and she added me on WeChat. She gave me a missed call and I saved her number. For the next ten minutes, we did what everyone does after adding a new WeChat contact – look at other person's moments (which is sort of like an inbuilt Instagram feed) and spy on each other's lives shamelessly. Her moment posts were mostly work related. My social media contents were more personal than work. This might actually be the biggest difference when you work for yourself versus when you work for others – you use your social media to grow your business rather than posting useless crap like food and travel photographs, the way I do.

Our breakfast arrived right about the time I came to the above conclusion, which helped avoid further awkward conversations. Nicole had ordered some red bean scones for herself along with hazelnut and coconut scones for me. We enjoyed a quiet breakfast, and the coffee helped clear some more of that fog in my head. In the back of my mind, something didn't really compute and I felt there was something definitely amiss here. Things like this never happened to me, period. I tried to push out the negative thought and tried to go with the flow.

We were unnaturally comfortable with each other when we were discussing life in Shanghai, which was very rare for me when it came to strangers. What I discovered as we ate was the fact that we were unnaturally comfortable with each other's silence as well, which was even rarer with me. I took a pause there and reminded me that, I was getting ahead of myself. I don't see a girl like Nicole would want anything to do with someone like me; I have learnt this from experience.

We ate in silence and continued to spy each other's WeChat Moments. Soon, there were a lot of likes popping up on my post, especially my photography posts. Most of Nicole's posts were in Chinese and there were some posts which I could understand and I liked those, mostly because I was pleased with my ability own to read some simple Chinese. There were hardly any photos of herself, except a few photos from team dinners. She appeared to be a very private person, who shared things very selectively from her personal life or I was overly social media dependant and Nicole was a normal person who didn't feel the urge to post everything from her life.

I finished the scones and waited for Nicole to finish the scones, which was less than half done by the time I finished the whole scone. She asked me if it was getting late for me. I assured her that I don't have anywhere to go and I am okay to wait until she was done with her scone. I could see that she was pleased with that response and continued to nibble on her red bean scone and sip her coffee.

Since we were being so friendly and I was no longer sleepy, I thought I should ask her why she reacted the way she did, on the train.

"Hey... Nicole, can I ask what happened on the train? I mean, you were pretty shaken up and if you want to talk about it, I am happy to listen", I inquired as gently as possible.

She looked at me with those beautiful liquid black eyes, but it felt as if she's trying to look into my heart and soul. Clearly, she was deciding what to say. For some reason, I knew that she wasn't angry at me and I knew that I hadn't screwed up yet. Something in her eyes conveyed that message. If anything, she was sad and I felt this wave of compassion for her. I wanted to hold her and tell her everything okay, and I would have done so if I knew her longer than three hours; I don't want to be seen as someone who takes advantage of a woman in a weak moment.

After what felt like an eternity, she sighed and said, "Let's talk about this when we meet for dinner, okay? I don't want to keep you waiting."

I knew from her tone that, she needed some time to compose her thoughts or she was politely telling me not to pursue that line of thought. I needed some sleep in any case, so I nodded in agreement and added, "Sure, let's talk about it whenever you feel like to talking about it."

"You told me that you will be shipping out the material, will you be doing that yourself?" I added, mainly to change the subject.

"Yes, just me", she replied, "I can do the packaging and call the *Zhongtong* guy to come and pick up the packages here." She sounded relieved that we changed the subject.

A thought was forming in my mind, but I had no idea how to express it properly. A cigarette would have really helped. She continued to nibble her scone and sip the coffee.

I took a sip of the lukewarm coffee, and asked hesitantly, "Do you need some help to do the packing? I have pretty much nothing to do, and if you don't mind, I can come over and help you."

"Hmm, let me think about it", she said. In China *'let me think about it'* generally meant, *'No'*.

"Didn't you say you are planning to do…" she quickly added with a tilt of her head trying to recall whatever I said "What did you call it… Ah yes, Metro Surfing? What exactly is that?"

I know, she wanted a subject change and I respected her desire not to accept my offer to help. A girl like Nicole must have literally hundreds of men falling over themselves to "help" her, especially in China where the sex ratio is as bad as it is in India. The average Shanghainese man does everything for their beloved wife or girlfriend (or both) and goes to great extent to keep their wife or girlfriend (or both) happy. They would buy apartments worth millions of RMB, cars, car licence plates and luxury good for their loved one. They are okay to cook, wash, clean, and do most of the housework to keep their respective wives happy. In comparison, an Indian IT guy who believes in gender equality and sharing responsibilities equally doesn't really stand a chance.

"Ah yes, during the Chinese New Year holidays, you know that most people would go back to their home, leaving large cities like Shanghai relatively empty" I started explaining and Nicole nodded her head in agreement.

"As I have pretty much nothing to do, and since the metro would be empty, I use this time to travel end-to-end on all 13 metro lines, the *Zhangjiang* tram, and the Maglev" I continued to explain, "It should take about 2 or 3 days. At the terminals stations of each of these lines, I would take a photo as proof of my journey."

As I started explaining my idea, I realized how silly it sounded when I said it out loud. Any normal person would use this time to travel around, soak in some culture, and get drunk with buddies at your favourite pub or something like that. But then… I have not been normal for a very long time. Nicole stared at me incredulously and I started blushing again. It felt as if, any moment now, Nicole would burst out laughing on my face.

"I don't think even the local Shanghainese people would have travelled on all metro lines, especially end-to-end", Nicole said, her face inscrutable, "I look forward to seeing those photos on your WeChat moments."

Even though her face was inscrutable, she sounded genuine.

"Sure, I will probably do this on the weekend before the *Chuxi*", I said, *Chuxi* being the eve of Chinese New Year's.

We both took a sip of coffee from our respective cups and, Nicole continued to nibble her scone. It was almost done… but she was so slow that I wanted to shake her by her shoulder and tell her "Just put that scone out of its misery!"

My phone vibrated in my pocket making me jump; I had forgotten about its existence.

"Excuse me", I said and took out my phone to see that there were 8 or 9 WeChat messages from Allen. For a good measure, he had messaged a couple of 'Dude, you there?' messages on WhatsApp and iMessage (which was the reason the phone vibrated). Apparently, he was under a lot of pressure from his wife to set me up with her friend for a coffee meet. His wife (apparently) felt that we are very suitable together and was pissed off at Allen that he didn't broach this subject with me, despite the fact that we hung out the whole night and despite her constant reminder.

There were a couple of 'Beautified' photos of the girl. The girl was very pretty, but then after meeting Nicole, this girl didn't even come close. I know… I am very superficial. Allen was one of the first friends in Shanghai and I owed him a lot. Also, the possibility of meeting a pretty girl like that is so low in my life that I agreed to meet her. Just to be done with it, if not anything else.

As soon as I sent the message, I put the phone in Do Not Disturb mode and laid it face down on the table, next to the coffee cup.

Meanwhile, Nicole had finished her scone was sipping the coffee, and was waiting for me to be finished with the message.

Chapter 8.   The Grass is Greener

"Why do you want to leave China? Don't you like it here?" Nicole asked me, very abruptly.

At first, I thought she was angry at the fact that an Indian didn't like China, but then it was more of a curiosity that I saw on her face.

The usual answer I gave people if they ask me this question was that I am heading back home and start something by myself. This answer was sellable, as I had enough work experience and I had an MBA from one of the best B-schools in China. You do an MBA, start a business, call yourself CEO, and throw around a few jargons… it is only logical. While I was considering which version to present, Nicole waited expectantly for my answer. My intuition told me honesty is the best policy.

"If you don't want to talk about it, it's okay", Nicole said sensing my hesitation.

"No, it's not that… The usual answer for that question is – I would like to go back to India to start my own business", I paused to take the last sip of the coffee and continued, "But the reality in short is, I am tired of being alone here, nothing more and nothing less. I am tired of all these… uh… short-term relationships. If I head back home, I have my parents, my sister, and my extended family to look forward to.

"Back there, I might even find that life partner that I have been looking for… Someone with shared background and culture. It's time, to be honest with myself, I might have been looking in the wrong places and might have been approaching this relationship thing all wrong… Plus I sort of miss home", I concluded hesitantly.

Whatever I said had struck a chord, as Nicole seemed genuinely surprised and her lips were parted in surprise. This must be her version of dropping jaw. The parted lips made her look like a model, getting ready for a shot. My throat constricted a bit at that image, and my heart skipped a beat. I gulped down that ball of emotions stuck in the throat, fake coughed into my balled fist and broke eye contact with her in the process. I prayed for her to close her lips or start talking. She looked even more angelic.

"I know how that feels!" she exclaimed finally, her face slightly flushed, "This is why I came back to Shanghai. I always felt alone no matter how many ever friends I had or how many other Chinese or Shanghainese people were there in Sydney. I hated the fact that I missed my family so much all the time. I hated how people judged me for being a woman and whatever I achieved, was attributed to my looks. I hated myself for getting into relationships with these so-called perfect guys who were, in the end, nothing but superficial and vain. It seemed like all they wanted was... sex and money.

"I wanted to become Australian so bad, but after that happened, I realized that I am more or less the same person. A friend of mine had told me once – *You can take me out of China, but you cannot take China out of me.* I used to laugh at her, but God knows she is right. I am Australian now, and I did it by myself, but apparently, that was not enough for me.

"I thought that living in Sydney was getting to me and moved to Melbourne, thinking the change would help. Not. One. Bit" she said, emphasizing each word. She paused for a moment, as if deciding how to put her thoughts into words, and continued, "I missed Shanghai and China even more. Don't get me wrong, I like being an Australian citizen and I like the fact that I have the freedom to travel anywhere I want, but home is home. Finally, after more than 12 years in Australia, I made up my mind to go back to Shanghai. I knew that I can find something to do in Shanghai, and in worst case scenario, I can live off my parents' money. They had loads of money in any case and they used to tell me often that I really didn't need to work", she paused and laughed at her own joke.

I smiled because she was genuinely happy, and not because her joke was funny – I didn't get the joke anyway.

She took the last sip from the cup and finished off the coffee. She studied the lip of the coffee cup for a few seconds. She seemed lost in some thought. I tried to see what she was looking at. Might be the outline of her lip balm. One instant, my eyes were focussed on the lip of her cup and in the next instant, my eyes focused on her lips. This was the first time I noticed that she had a tiny mole on the right side or her lips. Before she snapped out of her reverie, I quickly looked down and pretended to study my fingernails. I didn't want to see the phone as I was scared of seeing more messages with more requests from Allen.

She finally let out a loud sigh and relaxed her whole body. I looked up and, she concluded, "To be honest, this business was something that just happened. I was in the right place at the right time. I know I shouldn't be laying this out on you but, it feels good to talk."

All this literally tumbled out, and I got a feeling that she had seldom talked about this. I am not sure why she felt she could talk about this with me and talk so much, but she was transformed completely and seemed free of tension. The sparkle in her eyes intensified to the point where I couldn't meet her eyes.

"Don't even mention it, I am glad that you could talk to me, a complete stranger", I responded with a smile while thinking – *Damn, I should have shared more*. Nicole excused herself and got up to go to the bathroom and I started thinking about what Nicole just told me.

After what I heard from Nicole, it did appear that the grass was not greener on the other side after all. Given the extremely average nature of my life and looks, I have always envied and admired attractive people. They just seem more confident and comfortable in their own skins. Come to think of it, attractive people have no choice but to be confident; their confidence is what makes them attractive. It might be a self-fulfilling prophecy for them.

I always felt that attractive people can never be alone, but after listening to Nicole, I could feel how lonely they could get. They might have people around them and they might have a well-practised smile on their faces, but inside they could be the loneliest of the people on earth. Agreed that everyone is different, and it's possible that Nicole is not really a representation of everyone, but I am sure that there are certain things that might be common amongst such people. What I realized is that they might be judged for everything they do – Their choice of a partner, their choice of friends, and perhaps even their choice of what they eat or wear. Their partners will never be attractive enough, their friends might not be true friends and their choice of foods or clothing seen as snobbish. It's truly a lonely place to be in.

When I said, I felt lonely, if I am honest to myself what I really mean to say is - *I don't have a girlfriend and my prospects of finding one are really low, no matter where I go.* In reality, I do have a lot of amazing friends in Shanghai and all over China, since I have lived here long enough. Most of them accepted me for the person I am, the rest of them outright loved me for my clumsy efforts to learn the language and the fact that I eat *FengZhua* or chicken feet every single time I go to a dim sum restaurant.

On the contrary, with Nicole, who was in my humble opinion, the representation of attractiveness, what I saw in that moment of vulnerability was a person who desires something I had, and I had not learned to cherish – a normal, average life. This was possibly just my feeling, but I also had a feeling that I was right.

For the first time since we met, I tried to look beyond her looks and the recently discovered fact that her family has loads money, both which were objectively the hardest thing I did in my whole life. I was born with the gift of self-awareness, and I was painfully aware of my capabilities and shortcomings. This helped me accept the fact that Nicole probably needed someone who's painfully self-aware to talk to so that the guy wouldn't start hitting on her. I let out a sigh as reality hit me with the force of a slamming door. At least I will not have too many false hopes; no more of that imagined 'comfortable with each other' crap. In my life, it was stupid to expect anything different.

Coming back to the present and the now, I was super sleepy, super tired and super deprived of nicotine. No amount of coffee or beautiful women was going to help me now. I needed some sleep. Nicole came back with a smile on her face which said one thing – she wanted to talk more.

"Nicole, it was really great talking to you, but I don't really want to hold you up. I will head back home now. Thank you so much for the coffee and scones, I feel like a new man", I told her standing up before she could start talking again. It came out too abrupt for my own liking... Damn my low Emotional Quotient!

She seemed sort of disappointed, but she recovered quickly. I had tried really hard to look perky and alert, but my bloodshot eyes and dark circles said a different story. She could see how tired I was with my sagging shoulders and grey face.

"You do look really tired," she said as she stood up and added "I don't want to keep you here for long, but I have not been able to talk to anyone the way I talked to you and it feels good. I like the fact that you are a good listener. If you don't have anything to do, can we meet tomorrow evening itself for the dinner? I would like us to talk more. I am thinking, we can go to the Blue Frog at 96 Plaza. We can meet here at, say 5 PM and share a ride", she concluded and waited for my response.

This time, my jaw didn't drop, but my thoughts went haywire for a couple of seconds. *I am a good listener!? That's called being dumbfounded*, I thought. Maybe it's my eyes... I have been told time and again that my eyes are way above average and exuded kindness, like a dachshund puppy.

"I am free tomorrow and yes... We can surely meet tomorrow for dinner", said I trying to suppress the ear-to-ear grin that was forming on my face. I was free on most evenings, why would she ever think that I have anything to do? Cracked me right up, but I managed successfully to suppress that grin down to a polite, albeit a bit tired, smile.

She didn't make any attempt to suppress her own happiness. She smiled an ear-to-ear grin and reached to give me a hug, and mumbled, "Thank you, Anand. You are very kind."

I hugged her back, and interestingly, I wasn't physically aroused by the hug. On the contrary, I felt protective of her and knew in that instant, this goes beyond normal physical relationship defined by hormones and known sciences. I had read somewhere that you spend a lifetime getting to know a person and still not know the person, and some other cases in some cases you get to know the person in an instant, instinctually. I might be wrong, but I knew in that instant that Nicole is a genuine person and I knew that we can be good friends.

I released her after two Mississippi and told her, "You are most welcome, Nicole."

She let go at the same time; perhaps she was counting as well. She walked to the door and opened the door for me. I stepped out of her apartment and pushed the lift call button. She stood there smiling and, as I got into the lift told me, "Take care Anand, rest well, and see you tomorrow."

"See you tomorrow", I called out as before I entered the lift and pressed the button for the first floor.

Chapter 9.   Heading Back Home

As soon as I stepped out of Nicole's apartment building, I fished out my cigarette pack, lit up a cigarette and started walked back home, which was about ten minutes by walk or five minutes by bike from Nicole's apartment.

I was more or less on auto-pilot and took me about fifteen minutes by walk to get to my apartment block. I was fairly certain that I looked like a zombie by the time I reached there, with dark circles under my eyes and an intense stare as I tried to focus on the world around me. I smoked one more cigarette outside the block in the freezing cold before heading up to my apartment, which was also on the thirteenth floor. What can I say? I am the "superstitious" types and wanted to see what happens if I lived on the thirteenth floor.

I entered my cold apartment, turned on the living room & bedroom room heaters to full blast and sank into the couch in my living room. My body relaxed as some of the tension and tiredness eased out my aching muscles. I looked around my sparse, yet fairly tidy one-bedroom apartment and realized for the first time that I really needed to spruce up the place. It was designed to be functional, rather than attractive.

As you enter the Spartan flat, you would notice a tiny dining area to the left and a small walk-in kitchen right next to the dining area, again to the left. The house owner was kind enough to install IKEA wall cupboards in the dining area that I used for storing my nuts, oats, protein powder, a couple of bowls & plates, some Rubbermaid and Tupperware boxes and some bare minimum cutlery. The kitchen was a bit crowded as I liked to cook whenever possible and was usually well stocked. On the right side of the entrance was an average sized bathroom, which had a basic washbasin, a western commode, an automatic washing machine above which rested a tiny tumble dryer and, next to the western commode was the enclosed shower area.

You would walk into a large well-lit living room once you cross the dining area and bathroom, which was furnished with a two-piece IKEA sofa set, coffee table and a TV stand (both again from IKEA). On the aforementioned TV stand rested one of my larger purchases, a Mi branded 55-inch 4K LED Smart TV with Mi branded sound bars. The house owner gave me a DVD player, by which was my pile of DVDs, which was the only thing that was not very well organized in my apartment. Beyond the living room was a four-square-meter balcony where there was a pulley operated clothesline, and a small foldable lawn table and chair from IKEA. The balcony faced the street, and beyond the street was the apartment complex that Nicole lived in.

The bedroom was on the right side of the entrance and right next to the living room and was the second largest space in the apartment. This space doubled up as my study as well. My landlord had provided me with a queen-sized bed, and two small nightstands. On the left nightstand was my old iPad Air, my Bose SoundLink Mini II, and a plug board with my iPhone charger. Right next to the bedroom door was a large closet. In the corner at the end, next to the window was my study space, which was a complicated computer table I acquired in one of the WeChat second-hand groups and an ergonomic swivel chair I got on discount at IKEA. My other big-ticket purchases were on the computer table, a 2015 13-inch MacBook air, a Bluetooth Keyboard, a Microsoft Designer Mouse and a 25-inch LED display from Dell. The MacBook will soon be replaced with 15.6 inches Mi Notebook Pro, as soon as my bonus was paid out.

The only real decoration in the whole house was a black and white panorama of the Forbidden Place.

So here I was, sitting on the couch and trying not to nod off. I needed to use the toilet, brush my teeth properly as there is only so much chewing gum or index finger brushing can help. I also could do with a shower and a scrub down as I was starting to smell... very musky, to put it politely.

I removed the extra layers of clothing, except the pullover, slipped out my jeans and slipped into my shorts. My shoes went into the shoe cabinet by the door and I slipped on a pair of loafers. I hung my jacket out on the balcony, and I piled the rest of the clothes into my washing machine. I needed a black coffee and cigarette before I can go to the toilet, so I paddled to the kitchen and made a cup of sweet instant coffee. I never smoked in the house, so I stepped out into the cold balcony to smoke a couple of cigarettes.

I set down the coffee on the coffee table, quickly lit the cigarette with my shaking hands and started smoking furiously. The steaming coffee gave some respite from the cold. Half-way through the second cigarette, I was ready. I finished the cigarette and coffee and headed back in.

I grabbed a towel on my way to the toilet. I turned on the heater in the bathroom, stripped off rest of the clothes and dumped all of them except my shorts into the washing machine. It was then noticed red bruises on either shoulder, the bag strap had bruised my skin and from the depth of its colour, it looked as if, the bruise should take some time to disappear. I looked at myself and thought *No hot shower today, need a cold shower to ensure proper muscle repair.*

I didn't have any time to admire myself; I really had to go to the toilet now. Five minutes later, I was done with my 'business' and leisurely brushed my teeth. I noticed that my stubble was a bit too long, but I decided that I can wait until tomorrow morning for that shave.

I turned on the shower faucet all the way to hot and let it run for a few minutes and turned it back to the neutral position to get a cold, but not icy cold, shower running, I had calculated the temperature to be at around 15-16 degrees. I hung the towel on the hook behind the door and stepped into the cold torrent. I felt the cold water cutting into my skin and let the tiredness seep out of my body. I let the cold-water flow over my sore shoulders and felt the pain and soreness easing off. I stepped out from under the shower to shampoo my hair and to scrub myself. I immediately started shaking and shivering as the cold hit me again, despite the fact the heater was running in the bathroom. I quickly shampooed my hair and scrubbed up my body with a soap bar before getting back under the shower again to wash off the suds.

As soon as I was done with the shower, I stepped out of the shower and dried myself off with the towel. I was shaking like a leaf and I allowed my body to get used to the cold. I wrapped the towel around my waist and made a beeline to my bedroom.

I quickly got into my sleeping gear – shorts and t-shirt and slipped under the quilt. I plugged in my iPhone changer to my phone, turned on the Bluetooth, paired it with my SoundLink Mini II and started playing Atomos. There were a lot of messages on the phone which I ignored. I turned off the Wi-Fi and cellular internet to ensure that I don't get any more messages. To ensure that I don't get disturbed by spam calls, I kept the Do Not Disturb mode on. My parents and close friends know that when they need to reach me, they would let the phone ring three times, disconnect and then call me again to bypass the Do Not Disturb. Others can wait.

As it was well past 11 AM now, I slipped on an eye mask to block out the light and turned into the right position for my sleep, which so happened to be sleeping on my right side. The combination of tiredness, the soothing music, and the eye mask was super effective and I drifted off into a deep sleep in less than five minutes.

PART 2 – WISE MEN SAY

Chapter 10.   The Cure for A Hangover

I was finally fully awake. It was around quarter to seven in the evening. I got out of my bed with a throbbing headache that I have been trying to ignore since about six PM. It was useless, no matter how hard I tried to go back to sleep, it was just impossible. It was like being in a limbo. It was also as if someone was playing the drums on my head with a hammer.

Everything was out of focus for half a minute. My stomach grumbled from all the acidity and bile. I needed coffee with a dash of Irish cream and a double cheeseburger with a side of fries, but none of that fast food crap, a good handmade burger, maybe at a Blue Frog or Beef & Liberty.

First things first, that coffee first... Maybe I should skip that Irish cream. Better to work up some sweat rather than get more booze into the system. Come to think of it, maybe I should skip the burger too. I should rather go and get some peanut sauce noodles from *Dingtele*, a local Shanghainese noodle joint that is as loved by the locals as it is hated by the outsiders. The place was budget friendly and healthier when compared to a double cheeseburger at the Blue Frog or Beef & Liberty. I was one of the few foreigners who regularly ate at *Dingtele* and the people who worked there knew what I liked to eat.

I made a coffee and drank it as quickly as possible without burning myself. I washed my face and brushed by teeth quickly. I ignored the phone, as I knew that the moment I turned the internet back on, I will get sucked into messages and news alerts.

I had a pull-up bar installed in my living room, to the chagrin of my landlord. I quickly slipped on a pair of gym shorts and my training shoes. I did a quick warm up and dived right into a circuit workout of 50 assisted pull-ups and push-ups in a pyramid of 20, 15, 10 and 5 reps. This was followed by a high intensity interval training of 100 sit-ups, 100 prisoner squats, and 50 burpees. I concluded the training with three rounds of planks and side planks

– one minute for the planks, 30 seconds each on both sides and 20 seconds of rest. Including all the breaks, it took me 45 minutes to complete. Not my best performance, but it was good enough to work up a decent amount of sweat. The hangover had settled down to a dull throb, and the nausea was history. I cooled down and mopped away the sweat using a gym towel. I was tempted to look at the phone and check all the messages, but I held back as touching the phone would delay me at least 15-30 minutes.

After about 10 minutes of cooling down, I went into my shower and took an icy cold shower that helped with some of the soreness in the muscles. The redness on either shoulder had faded a bit. Looks like the recovery should happen quicker than expected. I stepped out of the shower and towelled myself dry, shivering all the while until my body 'normalized'.

I dressed up quickly and layered myself with enough clothes to ensure that I don't freeze on the way to the noodle joint. I grabbed a thick jacket from my closet and my bag next to my study table as I headed out. It was about quarter past eight and I decided against biking to the metro station as I was not sure if I can get the last train back home.

As soon as I got out of my apartment block, I put on my earphones, started playing some music and broke into a jog towards metro station. I loved the feeling of the crisp Shanghai air breezing rushing past my face. I inhaled deep and burst out into a sprint; I ran flat-out for 30 seconds, before slowing back to a gentle jog. The heavy breathing forced more oxygen into my bloodstream, which helped push out any last remnants of hangover out of my system.

About five minutes later, I was at the metro station, feeling a bit out of breath, and I was thinking *I need to quit smoking*. I passed through the security and entered the metro station in time to get a train heading towards people square. The train was surprisingly empty, and I found an empty seat. It was time to check all the messages now. I turned on the Wi-Fi and cellular internet on my phone and connected to Shanghai metro's 'Peanut Wi-Fi'. I also turned off Do Not Disturb mode. The moment the phone connected to the Wi-Fi, an avalanche of messages and notification hit the phone.

I cleared all the notifications and opened up WhatsApp to check all my 'international' messages. There were a few messages in my family group and MBA group, but no personal messages or nothing I really needed to bother with. All was well internationally, at least in my little slice of the world.

I checked my text messages next. There were a few promotional text messages from my banks and the telecom company, again nothing that I really needed to pay attention to. I took a few seconds to mass delete some of the old messages that have been accumulating in my inbox since forever.

I finally turned my attention to WeChat, which had around 30 unread notification, and this excluded the group messages which were all muted. There were few personal messages from a couple of friends, but most messages were from Allen and Nicole. There were also three pending friend requests as well. I started going through all the group messages first. The international MBA group had a heated discussion around the contrast between US politics and China politics. Being an Indian, I had no dog in that fight. Plus, politics bored the life out of me. Personally, I was partial towards one party politics as it seemed to reduce a lot of management overheads and given that the US just elected a controversial undiplomatic president, I was not sure how people could still talk about merits of US politics, but I kept my opinions to myself. I didn't want to go poke the hornets' nest and get stung in my ass (because I am running away). My MBA class group was busy with messages about our upcoming reunion party. I checked the messages to confirm that the reunion party was indeed free and signed up in a jiffy. An Indian never misses a free party, doesn't matter if he or she has immigrated to a different country or if he or she is only part Indian. As long as there is some Indian in you, you are bound to be there. Just a personal view though, and really not a generalization.

The second-hand group that I was part of and sometimes moderated had some fun going on with some Indian guy calling out some Chinese guy trying to sell an ancient MacBook air for nearly USD 600. Some other Chinese guy had come out in support of his fellow Chinese and claimed that price was "reasonable for a laptop in mint condition and is 90% new", and the Indian was throwing tantrums as the laptop "was over 5 years old, and how the hell can it be 90% new". I wanted to support the guy, but he seemed unbalanced and was posting photos and screenshots from Chinese second-hand sites like ganji.com to prove that USD 600 was a rip-off. I guess it did prove his point, but I hoped that he chilled out a bit and took life less seriously. I silently wished him luck and cleared out the messages from the remainder of the chat groups which were either in Chinese or were not interesting for me.

There were a few broadcast messages with Chinese New Year messages. I copy pasted the same reply to all the messages – *"Wish you the same. Gong Xi Fa Cai :-)"*. You reap what you sow. One of the messages had my name in it, so I typed out a personal message – the above message with the recipient's name in it – and I ensured that the smiley face was there at the end of the message. A smiley face in a message makes everything better. Type a sarcastic or snide reply to some stupid message and add a ':-)' at the end. *Voila*! Message looks much better than the original message.

Finally, I was down to the messages from Allen, Nicole and the three new friend requests, but according to the recorded announcement, the train was just pulling into the people square station. It was around half-past eight now and quite a few passengers made toward the exit. I locked the phone, put my backpack, got out on to the platform and started walking towards the line 1 or the red line platform.

The walk to line 1 platform was lonelier than what I was used to, not the peak people's square crowd where everyone is stumbling and pouring over each other. If I am on time to get the train back home, I am sure that I can see the rush to get the last-minute train. Come to think of it, might as well try to get the last train couple of trains. I remembered that the metro service was extended by half an hour on the weekends, *Yay*. One of the signboards along the interchange corridors did confirm the last train is indeed 30 minutes later on Fridays and Saturday. This meant that I can most possibly make the last train back home.

This is good news for me. I always do a time-lapse video of getting out of line 1 and transferring to line 2. Today I can do that, and share onto WeChat, Instagram and Facebook. What can I say? I am a "like monger". That reminded me that I need to check my Instagram and Facebook as well. With that happy thought, I had reached the Line 1 platform.

The metro TV confirmed two things, that I have to wait for about 2 minutes for the train towards South Huangpi road station, and that the metro service is in weekend mode and is extended by half an hour. In a place where English is rarely spoken, and where your local language skills are at best basic, it is always better to safe to be double sure.

I unlocked my phone again and opened WeChat. I looked at the invitations and two of them were my MBA School's new intakes – They probably added me from one of the MBA groups. I accepted their request knowing very well that they might be only connecting with me as they are looking for internships or jobs, not that I could really help them. The third one was from a lady I didn't recognize. Like some of the Chinese people, she didn't use her name to identify herself and had used some phrase that was supposed to make them look "intelligent", I guess. To confuse the poor foreigner more, instead of a full-face profile, she had a photo taken from behind with her facing the sun, so all you can make out is the silhouette – This usually means they think they are beautiful and are worried that bad men will bother them by adding them. Thankfully, there were three greeting messages in English and that made me feel slightly better.

```
Strange Phrase in Chinese (WeChat):
Hi, I am Alice Wang.
```

This was the first greeting. This was sent at about 1 PM.

```
Strange Phrase in Chinese (WeChat): I
am Allen's wife Jean Li's friend,
Nice to meet you
```

Said the second greeting. This was sent at around 2 PM.

```
Strange Phrase in Chinese (WeChat):
Ok, maybe you are busy, message me
when you have time
```

That was the final greeting sent at around 3 PM.

Interesting... It almost looked like she was waiting for my response.

I accepted the friend request immediately and texted her back.

```
Anand Nair (WeChat): Hi Alice, thank
you for adding me. Yes, Allen did
tell me about you. I was sleeping
when you messaged me. Very nice to
meet you :-)
```

I didn't wait for her reply and went back to other messages. I was scared of what Nicole messages had to say. What if she had texted to say something like "Sorry, but something came up, can we meet later?" or something worse like... "I don't think we should be friends as I'm attracted to you", so I checked Allen's messages as I got into the train that just arrived at the platform.

Allen's had sent nine text messages, starting a couple of minutes past 11 AM. I might have just missed his message. First message thanked me for "dragging his ass back home"; Second and third message cursed me for 'borrowing' his Irish cream AND not cleaning the coffee mug, as his "A'yi is on leave"; Fourth and Fifth messages requesting my permission to pass on my contact to Alice; Sixth, Seventh and Eight messages were "Dude, you there"; and Ninth and final message, which he sent at around quarter to one, said "Wife kicking my ass, sending your details to Alice, sorry, and good luck buddy."

Sorry and good luck? What should I interpret from that one? Should I have not accepted the request from Alice? With that stimulating thought going through my mind, we reached South Huangpi road.

I got out of the train, swiped out of the metro and walked to the Exit 3 of the station. There were a couple of third-generation Mobikes, with adjustable seats, but I was not sure if I can ride on East Jingling road. Instead, I started walking, on Middle Huaihai Road, towards the noodle store.

Since I was walking at a brisk pace, I didn't look at the phone, despite the fact that I felt two or three vibrations indicating I've got messages. I didn't want to go crash into some old Shanghainese uncle or auntie and become liable for their injuries. I also didn't want to get injured myself as some of these old Shanghainese uncles and aunties are strong and energetic folks, capable of flash dances after eating copious amounts of braised pork and meat dumplings.

I soon reached this noodle place which was introduced to me by a friendly finance intern in my previous company, about seven years back or so. She had taken me there for a local dinner, which we had to follow up with some famous Shanghainese brand ice cream we bought from a nearby convenience store.

On our way back home, she showed enough skin and dropped enough hints as to what she wanted. Despite the fact that she was fairly attractive and oozed sexiness in every step and word, I refused the offer, as I had a strict no dating or relationship at work policy. She left the company afterwards and had remained in contact for a year or so after that. We then drifted apart as our lives became busier and more complicated over time. That was over seven years back. As you can see, the noodle place came with a side dish of personal history too.

The lady at the counter recognized me and greeted me with a friendly banter about still being single. I think she doesn't realize the fact that even if I have a girlfriend, I didn't want to bring my girlfriend to a hard-to-find hole-in-the-wall noodle joint. It should have been obvious, but then "obvious" is dependent on the culture you are in. Perhaps for the Chinese, it's normal to bring their girlfriend to this place, given that it was voted as one of the top ten lane house noodle joints. I guess, I still have a long way to go, in terms of learning the language and the culture.

In any case, I smiled and responded that I don't have an apartment yet, nor a Shanghai licence plate so can't find a suitable girlfriend. She nodded understandingly and asked me if I am going to eat the same thing – Peanut sauce noodles, fried steak and boiled lettuce? I told her that I had too much to drink last night so no fried steak and that I wanted less noodles and extra peanut sauce. The bill came to around RMB 20 which I paid up in two tens. I picked up the chopsticks and napkins, give the stub to the server Ayi and told her that I will be sitting upstairs.

I walked up the steep stairs to the "second floor", which was more like a mezzanine they had built to accommodate extra customers and was divided into two sections. There was only one guy in the first section and a girl in the second section. Nice, I can have a peaceful dinner, without being disturbed. The phone had vibrated a couple of times more, reminding me that I needed to see those messages. I got to grow a pair, stop imagining what Nicole might have said, and actually see those messages. I don't need to overthink this; my intuition said that she needs a friend and that she wants nothing more.

I chose a table that was the furthest from the girl. I dragged the table out so that I can slip into the inside seat. The table squeaked a bit and I could make out from the corner of my eye that the girl was looking up at me. I had this sense of déjà vu, something familiar about the girl, but I was so caught up in the thought of messages from Nicole and Alice that I didn't really give it any second thoughts

Chapter 11.   So Jaded...

"Is that you Anand? Oh my God! It is you! Why don't to you join me?" exclaimed a familiar voice as I started taking off the jacket. I was startled a bit as I didn't expect to meet anyone here, especially at this time. I know that voice anywhere. After all, she introduced me to this place seven years back.

Jade Lin. The sweet, attractive, and sexy intern who introduced me to this place and tried to seduce me with peanut noodles and Shanghainese ice cream. I swear I get aroused sometimes when I think of peanut noodles. She was there, waiting for her food order, apparently. She had aged well over the past seven years, she looked really good for someone who was around 30 or 31. Looks like Nicole and perhaps Alice's messages will have to wait. She had slipped out her seat and thrown open her arms to give me a huge bear hug. I hugged her right back. She smelled like heaven, a heady mix of her natural scents, expensive perfumes and creams.

"Hi Jade", I mumbled into the silky hair and cradling her head, "How are you? Long time no see!"

I didn't know that we were still on hugging terms, but I was not complaining. I started counting "Mississippis" and decided I should let go after three to five "Mississippis". I did genuinely miss her, and I wanted to reach out to her more than once, but I heard she had got married or engaged or something like that. Perhaps, I heard wrong. I lost count after five Mississippi's. She finally let go after about fifteen seconds, way longer than expected. She had a huge smile on her face and her eyes were sparkling with joy. That cannot be made up, unless and until she was high.

"I am okay.... God! I missed you so much", she said gazing into my eyes, and continued, "In fact, I was thinking, I wish I could meet you one of these days, and here you are! I was thinking of talking to Charlie Xie to get your number or WeChat. Forget that... Give me your number and WeChat right away. It looks like you changed your number. Let me give you my new number, I had changed my number about four years back."

I was touched by her enthusiasm and... a bit aroused. *God! Have I become a pervert?* I told her my number and asked her to give me a missed call. I could feel the phone vibrating. I unlocked my phone to save her number. I dismissed all the WeChat and WhatsApp notifications which were piling up now.

"I missed you as well. My phone number is my WeChat. You can add me from the contacts directly", I told her as I was saving her number. "In fact, I was thinking of you on my way here", I added with a wink and cheeky smile. I put my phone back into Do Not Disturb mode, locked it and put it into my pocket.

"Anand! You are so bad. I was so immature that time", she exclaimed and punched me playfully on my shoulder. She had blushed to a deep red as she understood the context perfectly.

She gave me another dazzling smile and hugged me again. It felt more purposeful than the first hug.

I could feel my arousal increasing and I hoped that she wouldn't notice. She did notice and didn't seem to care, I could feel her pressing closer to me, ever so briefly, before letting me go. I am not sure why I did, what I did next but I did it. I bend down, raised her chin and gently kissed her on her left cheeks, as close to her lips as possible. A very friendly kiss indeed, a high-five kiss. I let her go and sat down at her table as if nothing had happened.

I was ready for the noodles now.

She stood there blushing again at my sudden forwardness and after a couple of seconds, slipped back into the seat with a happy smile on her face. This would have been the weirdest thing that must have happened in this restaurant, and I was thankful that place was mostly empty.

"Let's finish the noodles quickly and get out of here. We can go to TGI Friday's or Element Fresh next to the bund. If you are not doing anything that is... let us get a drink, and catch up", she said as her order arrived. She had ordered peanut sauce noodles and boiled lettuce, as well. I confirmed with her that I had absolutely nothing planned for the evening but catching up on some writing I have been doing, which can wait.

As she was mixing her noodles, my noodles had arrived and I asked the Ayi there to get me some sesame oil or peanut oil. She got me some sesame oil. I added a tablespoon of sesame oil and mixed the peanut sauce into the noodles. I added a couple of spoonsful of the soup to loosen up the noodles and mixed the whole thing again. We started eating quietly while occasionally stealing glances at each other. It looked like she really wanted to ask me something.

The noodles tasted awesome and I was hungry. This bowl of noodles was not going to last very long.

"I don't mean to be rude, but I got to ask... Are you seeing someone these days?" Jade asked me finally, as I finished off the last of the noodles and vegetables. She was barely half-way into her noodles.

"Nope", I said shaking my head, "I am single now". I thought it would be obvious that I am single, by the fact that I am eating peanut noodles in a hole in the wall restaurant on a Saturday night.

I was not sure if I should ask her if she was single or not, but perhaps I should have asked her that question before boldly kissing her, even though it was a high-five kiss. We all know, there is nothing really called a high-five kiss.

"I am single too", she said almost as if reading my mind. She hesitated a bit and added, "Actually, I am divorced."

Why is she giving me this information?

"Oh... Okay... I am sorry about that", I asked instead. She didn't see too upset or broken up about it, so I added, "It seems we have a lot of catching up to do. Finish your noodles and let's get out of this place", I said playfully, trying to lighten up the mood.

She ignored me and continued eating her noodles leisurely. If she was upset about me trying to play down her being divorced, she hid it with a faint smile. Perhaps she was feeling happy at that moment. I let my eyes discretely roam over her, and if she did notice it, she ignored it.

Jade was short, around 5'2" – 5'3" tall, and had a curvaceous body, that was surely the envy of any average Chinese girl. Despite the curves, she looked healthy and fit. Her silky hair was kept long and it framed her round face with large pale brown, almost fawn coloured shiny eyes, her sharper than your average Chinese nose and full tiny pouting lips that begged to be kissed. Her chin was sharp and perfect. Again, way out of my league, but she was interested in me once upon a time.

If I remembered correctly, she had a mixed-blood heritage; her father is an Italian and her mother is half Han Chinese and half Hui Chinese. Her skin was pale cream coloured and I am sure it would feel like velvet or satin to touch. Although she was technically an Italian citizen, she had grown up in mostly China after her parents had separated. This happened when she was young and apparently, her father didn't want the liability of a child. This is the other thing I remember from the first time we had a meal together, which was at the same place.

She was done with her noodles and left about a third of it uneaten. This is why I always ordered less, they give too much noodles here and most people end up wasting the noodles. She dabbed clean the corners of her mouth with a nap, drank some hot tea to wash down the noodles and said, "Let's go".

I couldn't help but stare at her red lip, which seemed redder than when I met her. This time, she caught me staring at her, but she didn't make a big deal of it and stared right back at me. I was caught in her gaze and her pale brown eyes held me captivated for few seconds.

I finally tore myself away from her hypnotic gaze and wiped clean my lips too. I drank some hot tea to wash down the last bits of peanut sauce and so that she doesn't see me swallow the huge lump forming in my throat. I start chewing a piece of gum and got up to go. She got up with me, slipped on her jacket which looked like a Burberry and starts following me.

As we climbed down the steps, I offer my hand to her for support, half expecting her not to take it. She took it, and I could feel her skin and it indeed felt like velvet. As our hands touched, a vivid image flashed in front of my eyes and I felt that stupid lump forming in my throat again. I quickly swallowed, pushed out that image out of my mind as we stepped out of the restaurant and out on to the street. The lady at the front desk was super happy to see me with Jade and called out a typical Chinese restaurant wishes for leaving customers, the loose translation of which would be "Walk Slowly. Come back soon".

Chapter 12.   Sparks in Xintiandi

We got out of the restaurant and on to the street but were still holding hands. For some reason, it appeared that we had trouble letting go of each other's hands. After a few seconds of staring into each other's eyes, I let go of her tiny well-manicured hands.

"Let's take a taxi there", she said, visibly swallowing the lump in her throat. She took out her phone and used to ride-hailing app Didi to hail a ride to go to Pudong. As she typed out the address, I caught a glance of the time, and it was nearly 10 PM. As she hit the confirm button, I took out my cigarettes, moved next to a smoking post and lit one.

She followed me, took out her own packet of cigarettes, some kind of slims, drew one out and lit it using a stylish jet flame lighter. She started staring at the road and continued smoking placidly. As we stood there smoking our cigarettes, she inquired where I was living these days and I told her I lived closed to Century Park and she replied that she lived close to *Dongchang* road.

A jingle played out confirming that her ride-hailing request has been accepted. She stopped staring at the road and started checking the details of the car coming to pick us up. She was still facing the general direction of the road.

I didn't know what to say as we waited for the taxi. I suddenly remembered that we didn't have to go all the way to the Bund, as we had the option of going to Element Fresh in Xintiandi.

"Jade, why don't we go to Element Fresh in Xintiandi instead of TGI Friday on the Bund? It much quieter there and I like the ambience better." I said casually as I flicked the ash off the cigarette.

"That's not a bad idea, I am okay with either", she said stumping out her cigarette. She thought for a minute and made up her mind "Let's walk to

Xintiandi and see if we can get a seat. Oh, let me cancel the ride".

We started walking along Middle Huaihai Road in the general direction of Xintiandi. As we walked, she cancelled the ride she had booked and I heard the sound of Alipay wallet as a fine was auto deducted from her account for cancelling the ride. I took a last drag of the cigarette before stumping it out.

She put the phone in her bag and added "and, Xintiandi Element Fresh is open very late… I believe till two in the morning."

This again was one of those occasions where I didn't have anything to say, so I said the only thing that came to my mind, "Okay, that's great."

I hated myself for not being fast talking or glib, for not being able to come up with a smarter response than 'okay, that's great', but that's who I was… Someone who gets dumbfounded at simplest of the things. There were many possible responses to that comment now that I had ten seconds to think about it.

There were so many things I wanted to ask her, starting with what she had been doing for the past few years, but I decided that it's better to wait until we were seated in the cosy confines of Element Fresh.

"Anand, hey, Anand… Where did you go? You seemed lost for a moment there", Jade said pulling at the sleeve of my jacket. I had zoned out thinking about what the appropriate response should have been. She was staring at me expectantly and I knew that I had to come up with a response to her question. *God, why do I put myself into situations like this?*

We had reached the over-bridge and we had started climbing the stairs, which was steeper than I remembered from before. I climbed them two at a time to keep up with Jade, who was fairly nimble. I decided that honesty is the best policy in this case.

"Uh… It's just that I feel that sometimes my communication skills suck… Big time" said I panting slightly from the exertion of climbing stairs and talking at the same time. I took a deep breath as we reached the first landing and continued, "I mean, I could have said something better than 'okay, that's great' to your last comment. You must think that I am retarded."

She laughed at this comment, "Anand, you always think too much. Trust me, I never thought you are retarded. You don't have to make up things to just for the sake of it".

She paused for a moment to think and added, "Agreed, you are not glib, but that's what makes you, you... Thoughtful, caring and honest... Too thoughtful sometimes. At least this is what I think I know of you."

"Yeah well, too honest sometimes for my own good", said I blushing at her comment.

"Better than being a lying, manipulative son... scum", she said with an unexpected vehemence and checking herself at the very last moment.

There was no comeback for that, so I took her advice and kept quiet. We crossed the over-bridge and as we walked down the stairs, Jade held my left arm so that she wouldn't lose her balance. Her hands were cold and I wanted to cup them between my arms and protect them, but I didn't want to take any more excess liberty with her.

As we crossed Danshui road, I discarded the gum in a trash can we passed by and lit another cigarette. She quietly took the cigarette from my hand and without any hesitation started smoking it. The way she smoked that cigarette, I knew that I was not going to get it back, so I lit another cigarette and started smoking. I was not sure as to why she wanted to smoke my cigarette and not her own. If she wanted to try my cigarette brand, she could have just asked or was she so lost in thought that she didn't realize what she was doing. Maybe she was just being lazy. I also wondered if it was some sort of signal of intimacy.

Stop overthinking this, I told myself to quieten all these random, unproductive thoughts, but it would be great to know what was going through her mind.

We reached Element Fresh at Xintiandi and we had to wait for about ten minutes before getting a table. We quietly smoked another cigarette. This time I lit two of mine and handed over one to Jade, which she accepted with a grateful smile. Her eyes sparkled brightly as she watched me smoke. After a few moments, she looked away and started watching people walking around. A lot of people were passing by, either going to get a drink or coming out on one of the pubs lining the street and most of them openly stared at Jade and completely ignored me.

She looked like some artist's work had come to life, and it was difficult not to stare at her. I remained invisible to most people around me.

When it was time to be seated, we both decided that it's better to sit inside as it was getting colder outside and we had smoked enough for the time being. I know, if we were seated outside, we will be tempted to smoke more and Jade must have agreed with me.

I held open the door for Jade. As she passed by me, I caught a whiff of perfume she was wearing and felt dizzy again. I quickly followed her to our table. Jade removed her jacket, as I pulled out the chair for her. She draped the jacket on the chair and moved in to sit down. I caught another whiff of her scent and nearly blacked out.

Grow up, man! Stop acting like a teenager, I admonished myself. As she sat down I leaned in a hair closer than what was needed and I caught the scent of her breath, and I started feeling aroused again.

I gathered myself quickly, remove my jacket, draped over the chair across from her and sat down. There was a strange expression on her face, which was flushed and her lips were ruby red now. Her irises were dilated and her breath sounded shallow. If I didn't know any better, she was either aroused or feeling cold. I went with 'feeling cold', although I was not aware of any science that supported that theory.

She MUST be feeling cold, I convinced myself… I had a tendency to sell myself very short, and I like to play it very safe.

I cleared my throat and called for the menu. The waiter materialized five seconds later, with two each of the food and drinks menus, which was unnecessary as I always ordered gin martini, Bombay Sapphire version with olives. He glanced at both of us, smiled at me and with a flourish, lit the candle on the table. Perhaps he could read the current situation better than I could myself.

"This is unnecessary," Jade said, after taking a sip of water, "I know what I want. I usually drink Viña Casablanca, Merlot."

"And, what about you sir?" the waiter asked in fairly decent English. I know it sounds funny when an Indian act as the judge for English standards, but then this is China.

"I will take a Gin Martini, shaken, Bombay Sapphire version with olives", I said closing the menu and placing it on the table. I added with a smile, looking Jade into her eyes, "I too know what I want."

Jade found this funny and perhaps caught the underlying meaning, as I could see that her blush was back.

"We will not be needing the food menu", she said to the waiter who removed the menus and disappeared quietly.

We fell silent again. I was not sure why she was silent, but I was quiet because I was not sure where to start. I was also terrified of saying something stupid. The place was filled with people – friends, couples, families – who all had something to talk. I was feeling the non-existent peer pressure. I decided I can perhaps start with something innocent like what she's been doing for the past seven years.

"For a guy who knows what he wants, you sure do pretend a lot", she said breaking the silence before I could. She said this with a naughty spark in her eyes and lopsided smile.

"If I don't pretend, I might say or do things that you may not like or you may not find acceptable, like when I kissed you tonight", I responded defensively, immediately regretting saying those words. "Listen, I didn't mean any disrespect when I did that, I was just so pleased to see you after such a long time", I quickly clarified. In my mind, I just made things worse and pictured her stomping out of here, with me chasing after her.

She didn't seem insulted, instead, she seemed genuinely pleased. Our drinks materialised by our side and the waiter disappeared after a polite nod of his head.

"That's the thing Anand, I am not insulted," she said while twirling her glass of merlot. I stirred the martini with the olives, waiting for her to complete her thoughts, but I felt she might follow it up with a 'but' clause. So, imagine my surprise when she tells me, "On the contrary, I am happy to see you too and I like the fact that you were so happy to see me too."

She took a sip of the wine and purred in appreciation. Her lips looked even redder and eyes were shining like diamonds. She gently licked her lips, and it looked deliberate to me. So, knowing very well that she will be looking to gauge my reaction, I pretended as if I was captivated by the olives in my martini instead of staring at her. I was also trying very hard to calm down my arousal. I took a sip of my martini and felt the crispy martini warm up my body. I sighed in satisfaction and sipped the martini again and ate half an olive. I loved the bitter-sweet taste of olives, especially in a gin martini. For a few seconds, I was oblivious to everything around me, but her voice brought me back.

"So, tell me, Anand, how you been? What you been up to, all these years?" she asked, "The last time we talked was six years back or so."

"Oh, you know... just living my life one day at a time. I work at a different company now", I said after clearing my throat. It appeared that Jade was waiting for me to continue so I continued my ramble.

"Okay so... I was getting tired of working all the time, so I decided that I should take a break. This was about four years back. My contract was sent to expire in about five months and I had to option to continue. You know how much my boss 'loved me'", I said emphasizing 'loved me' with an air quote.

"Oh Yeah, I remember how much... whats-his-name 'loved you'", she said, air quoting 'loved you'. She was giggling hard, I think, trying to remember the name of my boss.

"Yes, Mr Ravi Kumar", I said laughing, "Yes, he 'loved' me a lot, so much that he would call me on weekend and give me 'urgent' tasks to finish", I said air quoting 'loved' and 'urgent'.

We both shared a laugh at the fond memory of a demanding, taskmaster of a boss, who actually cared a lot about the wellbeing of his people.

"I always wanted to do my MBA, but I wanted to ensure that I had the bird in my hand... I mean at least one admit in my hand. I didn't want to renew the contract, then put in the paper and let down Kumar", I continued as soon as we had recovered.

"Oh my God, you were worried about Kumar's feeling; how sensitive of you!" Jade said with a laugh and a wink.

"Okay, very funny... In any case, I had three months to get a decent score in GMAT and finish my applications. I was targeting CEIBS and HKUST since I have been living in China for four years already and it made sense to me", I didn't know why I disclosed that information as it didn't seem relevant. Strangely enough, Jade was captivated by my boring narrative. I was not sure if I should disclose the fact that I was dating a Chinese girl then, and I was sort of serious about her. I discovered very painfully that she was not as serious about the relationship as I was. Another sip of the martini helped me decide that I better not disclose the details of that relationship, as that was one burnt bridge I was not really proud of.

"I registered to take GMAT two months down the line and for the next seven weeks I woke up at 4 AM every day, studied for the test. I used every available free time, including my lunch hour preparing my MBA applications, studying for the test and convincing my managers, including Kumar, to give me sparkling recommendations" I continued and Jade seemed to be hanging on to every word I spoke. Her smile and a slight nod of her head motivated me to continue, with my story. I noticed that her wine glass was empty, so I signalled to the waiter, who magically reappeared next to us, to get her another glass of wine.

When her wine arrived, she took another sip of the wine and I followed her suit. I took another sip of the martini I have been ignoring for so long, ate an olive and continued with my story.

"All the effort paid off as I managed to get a decent, above average GMAT score. That combined with my work experience and the recommendations, got me into CEIBS, but not into HKUST. This was okay for me as I thought I had my life figured out, and CEIBS was closer to home for me", I shouldn't have disclosed the last part as I could see her eyebrow going up, in slow motion.

"Closer to home?" she asked questioningly, took another sip of the wine and licking her lips deliberately.

I hate it when I dig my own hole and keep falling into it. There was no way out of this one, so I finished my martini in a gulp, ate the remaining olive, and ordered another martini before I continued with my story. I asked for extra olives this time.

"Listen, if it is something you don't want to talk about or something you are not proud of, you can skip over it, but you can talk to me and I am not going to judge you", she said as we waited for my martini with extra olives to be served.

"No, it's fine. I just don't talk about it anymore", I said lying to myself as much as I was lying to her.

My martini with the extra olives materialized in front of me about ten seconds later... ten seconds that we spend staring at each other. I was trying to figure out how much I can trust her with. There was something in her eyes that I couldn't place, but then my emotional quotient was fairly low and whatever remaining emotional quotient I have, nosedives after a couple of stiff drinks.

I need some liquid courage before I could continue with the story. I ate two olives and took a large gulp of the martini finishing about one-third of the drink in the process. Jade took a large sip of the wine that nearly finished half her drink. I did what any gentleman would do and ordered a bottle of the merlot and I asked for an extra glass so that we can share the bottle. To hell with not mixing drinks. I felt this was the right thing to do when there is going to be digressions in the story. The waiter refilled Jade's glass and poured me a glass as well. I ignored the wine for the time being.

"I was in a serious relationship that time, which I thought meant something and I wanted to stay in Shanghai for that person. I am not saying there is anything wrong with CEIBS, but if I was not in a relationship, I would have probably been more serious about HKUST and would have applied to other universities as well. She left me halfway into my MBA, as she wanted to, in her own words, think of her own future, and she was not convinced I could give her a future that she wanted, as I am an Indian. Anyway, that's all in the past." I concluded keeping all emotions out of my voice. But, if I am honest with myself, it hurts a lot – having failed so miserably a second time in a relationship and having to talk about it. I still didn't know the real reason for as to why my ex-girlfriend left me.

I could see a mix of pity, empathy and sympathy in her eyes as I told her this. I hated it when people took pity on my past. I took another large sip of the martini and paused to bring my seething emotions under control.

"Anand, I am sorry that you have to relive your past but trust me when I tell you this – you are better off single than with a person who cannot accept you for who you are – Indian and all", she said, in an attempt to pacify me. She took another large sip of the wine and waited for me to continue.

I finished the martini and the olives before continuing.

"Please... It's alright. I am okay to share this now", I said, swallowing the big lump of emotions forming in my throat.

"It looks like everything worked out okay... It seems like you are better off now", said she taking a large sip of the wine. If I didn't know better, she was trying to get drunk and get me drunk as well.

"Yup, you are right. The break up motivated me to study and work my ass off. I also managed to land my current job", I said nodding my head and pouring a large drink of wine. I also topped up her wine glass and she nodded her head in appreciation.

"So, all is well that ends well... I think you are doing better. You look better than ever", said with a hint of a smile on her face. She was twirling her wine glass and her eyes were bright. She seemed to be challenging me. My head was swimming from the martini, wine and all those pheromones. I was aroused, physically and mentally. I told myself that I was imagining things and drinks the drinks must have got to me.

"Yes, indeed", I said clearing my throat, "So tell me what you been up to?"

"Hmm... where do I start?" she pondered taking a large sip. Her speech was slurring a bit from all the wine. I decided to pace myself and took a small sip of the red wine and savoured the flavour and texture of the wine.

"Tell me, what do you do now?", I asked her trying to get her to talk. I intentionally avoided the subject of divorce.

"I work for an Italian conglomerate as a finance controller. I am in charge of the Asia Pacific business unit", she said, sounding bored, "but, I am serving my notice period now. My estranged father left me a fortune and his estate, so I plan to take a break and take care of some unfinished family business. I would like to do nothing for some time and catch up on my life. I was so busy with the work that I had a fairly successful career, but mostly nothing else."

She paused to take another generous sip of the wine. She licked her ruby red lips and contemplated as to what to say next.

"That sounds amazing. I wish I can do that. I envy you", I said abruptly.

"Haha, maybe you should do it", she said with a laugh and wink.

I laughed at that thought. If I had a bunch of cash or inheritance, I would use that money to travel the world and experience different cultures. I would love to try different kinds of foods and wines from these places. It will be good to have Jade with me, and we can travel and Airbnb all over Europe. I would make love to her every night. It would be amazing…

"Anand", she called snapping me out my little muse, "where did you go again?" she asked me while twirling the wine glass.

"I was just fantasizing… imagining", I said, quickly correcting myself – I don't want to use words that convey my true feelings. I continued, "I was imagining what I will do if I had a bunch of money. I will probably take a road trip around Europe, stay Airbnb and try different cuisines from around Europe."

"That's a good plan, we should do it", said Jade taking another large sip of the wine. I topped up her glass and pretended to ignore her 'we should do it' comment. She was getting drunk and was surely not in control of her thoughts.

"I mean it, Anand, we should totally do it. Don't think I am saying this because I am slightly drunk. I know Europe pretty well and I can be your guide", she continued, sounding somewhat in control but not entirely there.

"Okay, sounds like a plan, I will think about it", I said trying to conclude the subject. Now that I was getting drunk, I wanted to know more about the divorce, but I didn't want to reopen any wounds.

She nodded her head in satisfaction and started swirling the glass. She took a large sip of the wine and unsteadily placed the glass on a fork. The glass tipped over and I managed to grab the glass before the wine spilt all over the table. Jade mouth was open in shock and embarrassment.

"Listen, I think we both had enough wine", I said moving her wine glass away from her and pushing away my wine glass. This time I could clearly read the embarrassment and shame on her face.

"Sorry Anand, I drank too much and drank too fast. I think I need a cup of coffee, maybe a latte", she said blushing a bit. She pushed the wine glass further away from her.

"It's okay Jade, we have all been there before", I said reassuringly. She looked fragile and vulnerable and I wanted to do nothing but hold her and reassure her that everything is okay.

I waved to catch the eye of the waiter, who was on the computer doing something. When he materialized by our sides, I ordered two cups of latte with extra shots of espresso. I knew that the Italian in Jade would appreciate the extra espresso shot. She smiled and nodded her head in confirmation.

"Thank you, Anand. How did you know that I take my latte with an extra shot of espresso?" she inquired.

"I didn't know. I just ordered for you, what I usually order for myself", I said with a slight shrug of shoulder and tilt of the head.

Jade smiled and excused herself to go to the bathroom. She was a little drunk and a bit wobbly, but other than that seemed okay. She walked confidently to the ladies' room. I knew for sure, she was okay as she didn't stagger into the men's room and she gracefully avoided a drunk gentleman, who sort of stumbled out of the bathroom and missed the step.

It was nearly midnight, and I was slightly tipsy. I wanted to get out of here and get a fresh breath of air. I called for the billed and paid the bill using WeChat. There was a just over a quarter of the wine left in the bottle. I had half a glass full of the wine as well. Jade's glass was just over half full as well. I could make the outline of her lipstick on the rim of the glass. For some weird reason, I started thinking about her lip and started imagining how it would feel to kiss them. The waiter came back and served us the coffee with little chocolate cookies on the side. I snapped out my reverie and nodded politely at the waiter.

Jade was taking her time, and I was done twiddling fingers. I reached for my wine glass and finished the wine in a couple of large sips. I stirred the coffee breaking the foam art pattern. I blew the steam and took a tentative sip of the coffee. It was scalding hot, so I set it back on the table and waited for it to cool down a bit. I was tempted to reach for my phone and read all the messages that were piled up by now. I didn't want to start now because I knew I can't resist replying to messages and I didn't want to be distracted around Jade.

Thankfully, Jade came back to the table, sat down and took a large sip of the wine nearly finishing the glass. I guess she forgot about drinking too much and too fast. I didn't say anything, because she looked like she needed a drink.

"Sorry... I know, I should not be drinking so much, but just got a horrible message from the ex-husband. I don't know how he got my number" she said with some passion and finished her wine.

"Hmm... I am sorry to hear that. Do you... maybe want to talk about it?" I asked her tentatively as I pushed the coffee cup towards her. Jade shook her head and that was that.

I took a sip of the coffee and took a bite of the chocolate cookie. Jade followed my cue and took a large sip of the coffee and sighed in satisfaction. She licked off the foam that was stuck on her upper lips, an action I found immensely erotic. Right now, even if she blew her nose loudly, I would have found it erotic. We enjoyed the coffee in silence. We didn't have to say anything and apparently, we both were okay with that. I finished my coffee over the next ten minutes or so and Jade soon finished the coffee soon after. We both ignored the remaining wine. She didn't touch the chocolate cookie; she was perhaps watching her figure.

"Do you want to leave now? I could really use a walk", she asked as she wiped her lips with the linen. She took a sip of the water and waited for my response.

"Sure, that sounds good," I said. "By the way, I paid the bill", I added, as I could see she was taking out her credit card and about to call for the bill.

"Hey, that's not fair! I invited you", she said pretending to be upset, but I could see that she was pleased that I was being a gentleman.

"That's okay, if you are so upset, you can pay next time we meet", I told her tongue in cheek.

She got up laughing and put on her jacket. I did the same and indicated with a nod of my head that I am ready to leave. The waiter who served us that night helped to open the door and thanked us for our patronage. I slipped a 100 *renminbi* note into his hand and thanked him for his service. Tipping might not be a custom in China and but as a foreigner, there are some liberties that I am allowed. Plus the guy looked like he was from the

Philippines.

We got out on to the pedestrian street in Xintiandi and turned right to take a walk. It was nearly half-past twelve in the morning but the place was still well lit and had a fair amount of people loitering around. The German bar next to the Element Fresh had some live performance going on and people were streaming in and out of the bar. Jade linked her arms with mine and leaned against my shoulder as we walked towards the end of the street. I read that as a friendly gesture and tried not to think too much about it.

"I wanted to ask you about the divorce, but then I don't want to reopen any wounds", I said as we walked aimlessly. She looked at me for a few moments trying to size me up and probably trying to understand my motive. She must have been convinced as she took a deep breath and started her narration.

"Well, you shared your story, so it's only fair that I do the same. This happened a year after I left the company we were working for. I was young and my idea of a relationship was very different that time. I wanted to marry a rich, handsome guy who had many apartments in Shanghai. I found such a guy and fought my way to his attention. Me being half Italian sort of helped... initially. I was a curiosity that attracted many suitors and my future husband was a competitive type who wanted to win my attention one way or the other. Finally, he did win or I let him win. After all, luxury gifts and expensive restaurants were a sure sign that the guy was a good catch.

"We got married six months into the relationship. He was good to me for all of three months after which he started cheating on me and started seeing his ex-girlfriends, who just wanted to get back with him despite the fact that he was a married man. This is one of the hard realities of being a rich man – There are women who are desperate to find a rich partner or a sugar daddy and will do anything to win the attention of that man. I tried hard to get him back but he was already bored of me and his curiosity for a mixed blood Chinese was sated. At this point, he wanted to be with me only for my passport and nothing else", she paused as we waited to cross the street.

As she was speaking we crossed over to the other half of Xintiandi and walked towards the mall at the end of the pedestrian street. I could hear jazz music floating into the street from the bar grill located on the left side of the street. There were few couples taking photos in front some temporary art structure in the square by the mall. There was also a group of young foreigners celebrating someone's birthday.

"Long story short, just a year into the marriage, I had no option but to file for a divorce. I didn't want to be with a person who treated me like an object and who was using me to get a passport. I had learnt my lesson; I got what I wanted – A rich, handsome husband, but that came at a great price. It took me nearly two years of fighting and suing to get free of that demon", Jade concluded with a heavy sigh that indicated true extent of the relief she felt.

We stood in front of the art structure which was shaped like a large monkey, indicating the arrival of the year of the monkey. It was about thirty feet tall and was mostly red. I found it fascinating as it appeared to be made with large Lego blocks. As it was lit from inside, the surrounding area was washed in a reddish light.

I turned to look at Jade and saw that she was washed in the light from the sculpture and had turned a monochromatic red. She seemed to be admiring the sculpture. Her eyes were glistening and she stood rapt in attention. I could see the fine mist of her breath coming out through her parted lips. She looked incredible… ethereal even, and I couldn't tear my eyes off her. I was feeling tipsy now as the crisp air sort of enhanced the high from martini and wine.

"What? Is there something wrong?" she said as she turned to face me and caught me staring at her.

"Oh… Uh… No, there is nothing wrong", I stammered as I was brought back to reality. "I think you look different in this light", I continued, pointing at the sculpture.

"Oh, 'good different' or 'bad different'?" she asked looking me my eyes. I could see that her eyes, which are naturally pale brown, were so dilated that it looked black. Was it attraction or just low light? I went with low light.

"It's a 'very good different'. You look… angelic. Beautiful in a different kind of way", I replied emboldened by my partially drunk state.

She blushed visibly at that comment and despite the fact that she was washed in the light from the sculpture and I could see her blush. I was not sure if it was because she was angry or because she was feeling abashed at the comment or because she was probably drunk. I decided to play it safe.

"Again, I don't mean any disrespect; I am honest when I am drunk", I said with an embarrassed smile.

"Anand, its fine…", she said, and added bashfully, "I like it when you are honest with me."

Was that a hint that I got from Jade? For some reason, my subconscious couldn't reject that idea. I somehow knew that moment that Jade felt some sort of attraction for me.

We stood there for some more time, arms liked and unaware of the time passing. Jade drew closer to me until we were standing shoulder to shoulder. I didn't care about the time and I didn't care who was around us; I was feeling content.

We finally started walking back after about five or ten minutes. We didn't have to talk and felt mentally connected, at least that what I felt then. We walked hand in hand till we reached the beginning of the Xintiandi pedestrian street and joined the long queue for a taxi at the intersection of *Taicang* Road and *Madang* Road. As we waited, it seemed that it was difficult for us to let go of each other.

"This queue is too long, let me try to hail a cab using Didi", she said abruptly. I let go her hand and she did the same. She took out her cell phone and tapped out her home address. She got a ride in the next minute or so. This might sound a bit chauvinistic, but I have found that good looking women always could hail a ride easily in Shanghai.

I was about to try my luck hailing at hailing a ride, when Jade stopped me and told me, "Listen, you can take the same car since we are heading in the same direction. I can tell the driver to drop you home after he drops me home."

"Okay, that sounds good, but you will have to let me pay for the ride", I said trying to sound chivalrous.

"Not going to happen, you got the drinks… This is the least I can do", Jade replied firmly, and with a hint of a smile on her face.

I accepted the offer with a shrug and polite nod of the head.

Vijay Menon

Chapter 13.   The Tango

As we waited, I lit two cigarettes and offered one to her. We stood there smoking our cigarettes in silence. I was very much lost in my thoughts. I was not a big believer of God or fate or destiny or any of those things, but somehow, it felt that my life in the past two days was playing catch up for all that it had missed. Maybe there is a God after all or some sort of higher power who realized that I was not getting my fair share of friendship and relationships. How else can I explain meeting someone like Nicole in the most unbelievable way possible?! How else can I explain reconnecting with Jade in most improbable places possible?! How else can I explain all this happening in less than two days?

An atheist would perhaps use some sort of advanced statistics and probability to prove that it is possible that this sort of thing will happen once in a million year to guy like me and the guy just happened to be me... Or for an agnostic person like me, this might be the proof that there is God.

I was optimistic that, I have at the very least a fabulous friend, in Nicole. I was fairly sure that I will have something more with Jade, though I was not sure how to proceed from here. This is how things happened in my life, the beginning is good and I get the ball rolling, but sometimes the ball hits a valley and loses its momentum. There were far too many occasions where I would have a lot to talk, but finally reach a point whereby the third date, I have nothing to say.

I took a long puff of the cigarette and turned to admire Jade again when I realized that she was talking to me or more accurately, was trying to talk to me.

"Sorry? What did you just say? I was not listening", I stammered in an apologetic voice.

"I was saying that" she repeated, a bit abashedly, and her words slurring a bit, "...that, I too, think of you whenever I eat peanut noodles". She turned away from me trying to hide her blushing face and continued smoking.

I could feel my heart skip a beat. I was sure that time stopped as well. Everything was frozen for a couple of seconds. I dropped my half-finished cigarette and moved closer to Jade. I turned her around by her shoulder, looked into her beautiful eyes and told her, "Jade, I am going to kiss you now".

I half-expected a slap.

One moment, her eyes were wide with surprise, next moment she drew close to me with a smile on her face. She dropped her half-finished cigarette, looped her hands around my neck, and with surprising strength pulled my face down until our lips were hardly a centimetre apart.

"What the hell took you so long?" she whispered half playfully, half seriously, and a bit drunk. I could smell the wine and passion in her breath. I understood what she meant; counting from the day we meet, it took us over seven years to do what we really wanted to do.

I needed no further invitation and I kissed her. Whatever guilt I had about kissed her when she was drunk, evaporated the moment my lips touched her lips. She responded to the kiss and our bodies were melded together in a heady symphony. We kissed fiercely and hungrily – A hunger that has been pent up in both of us for seven years and a hunger that survived all the relationships and flings in between. Our lips and tongue were duelling passionately trying to satiate that hunger. The whole world around us along with 24 odd million people in Shanghai had ceased to exist for us – we were in our own little parallel universe, where we were together and we were happy. Nothing in the world could break this moment, nothing but the call from the car driver who accepted Jade's ride. Damn! I wish she had put her phone in Do Not Disturb mode.

We broke the kiss hesitantly and stood there looking at each other, a bit dazed, but basking in the heady glow of hormones and pheromones rushing through our body and dizzying our senses. We were like two magnets kept apart by force; we wanted to touch each other, taste each other, and consume each other in every possible way imaginable. I certainly had a wild imagination, but the first thought was – *I want to take her home and make love her.*

She answered the call and told the driver where we were waiting.

"Let's go to my place and uh... get some coffee there", she said hesitantly, with a slight blush on her face. Before I could protest, she added, "I am not asking you because I am drunk and senseless. I am asking you this because I want... this. I want to spend more time with you."

I hugged her again and gave her a gentle kiss. I could feel her passion by the way she was holding on to me.

I gently let her go and felt her hesitation in breaking the hug. I lit a couple of cigarettes and offered her one. She accepted it and started smoking with a look of satisfaction on her face.

The car arrived about a couple of minutes later and we stubbed out the cigarette, before getting into the car. I opened the door for her and watched her slide into the car gracefully. I got in beside her, and sit next to her, shoulder to shoulder, and cupped her cold right hand in my hands to warm them up.

"Oooh... your hands are nice and warm," she cooed, as she cuddled closer to me. For some weird reason, however cold it was outside, my hands always remain warm. It was weird because I am South Indian who grew up in hot South India and my body was technically supposed to be sensitive to cold.

Either the driver was in a hurry or sensed we were in a hurry. Whatever was the case, the driver drove like the devil and got us to her place in less than fifteen minutes. We didn't talk for the whole duration and did nothing but hold hands and feel each other's presence. The silence was heavenly and the air heavy with promises.

We got out of the car and on the street facing her apartment. Another jingle from her phone confirmed that the payment was deducted automatically from her account. She flicked the little button on the side of her phone to silence it and put the phone in Do Not Disturb mode.

She lived in the DongChang road area, and the apartment she lived in, was a walk-up apartment; one from before that area boomed and became one of the most expensive real estates in Shanghai. I follow her to her apartment building. She entered her six-digit passcode to unlock the main door; I turned away, to give her privacy.

"It's your birthday", I heard her say.

"What?" I asked a bit confused. My birthday was quite some time back at that moment, my brain was not really computing well.

"I mean the passcode has been your birthday since my mother and grandparents gave me this apartment around five years back", she repeated with a smile.

This hit me on many levels; it appears that I had mistaken Jade's forwardness, way back then. She perhaps was interested in me as a person as well. It was clear that she was interested in a physical relationship, but maybe, she expected a bit more than just mindless sex. It would also appear that she held me in a special place in her heart, which sort of affected me. Don't get me wrong, I still wanted to sleep with her, but I decided that I will do my best to be respectful. The assumption here, of course, was that all this will lead to sex, sometime soon.

As we walked up the stairs, I took out my cell phone, made a note of her address. I will send her a big bunch of flowers some other time. We reached her apartment, which was on the fourth floor.

"Are you okay?" She asked me, as she opened her apartment door with a traditional key. It was clear that a bit concerned with my silence.

"I am okay. Jade, I was wrong to judge you back then." I admitted to her, as we stepped into her apartment. I knew very well that she might ask me to leave. Before she could say anything more, "I am very sorry for that. I just realized how much I like you and perhaps..." I hesitated a bit but decided to say it anyways "...how much you like me, how much you think of me and how you think of me."

The last sentence came out really weird and was totally out of place. Even to my own ears, it sounded a bit narcissistic. Talk about bad timing. Her eyes widened a bit in surprise and smiled at what I blurted out.

"It's okay. To be honest, I was immature, superficial and shallow at that time. It took a painful marriage for me to become a somewhat normal person", she said, apparently lost in some painful memory. She closed the door behind us, turned on the light and heater and added: "I have always liked you for the person you are."

We stared at each other at this admission. I had forgotten about Alice completely and Nicole was just a faint but persistent memory. The silence was tangible, and we could hear each other's heavy breaths. I could feel the slight hum of the heater as the apartment warmed up slowly.

"May I have something to drink please?" I said breaking the silence. I know it's rude to ask for a drink at someone else's place, but I sounded much better than my real thought was, *I want to make love to you all night.*

"Oh… okay. I am sorry, I was thinking of something else" she said breaking the eye contact. She walked into her kitchen as I waited in her living room. It was a large living room which was similar to my living room in design except larger and had wine cabinet with a collection of wines. I recognized Yellow Tail, and Jacob's Creek, as these were the only wines I bought. If you don't know anything about wine, buy Yellow Tail or Jacob's Creek. Coming back to her living room, it also opened to a covered balcony with and I could make out an easel and a partially completed painting. This is another discovery for me – that she's interested in art. I should plan a visit to one of those art streets in Shanghai with Jade.

As I waited for her, I took off my bag and placed it near one the sofa.

Jade has returned with two wine glasses. She placed it on the living rooming coffee table. She took off her jacket and placed, in a closet next to the entrance of the apartment. I followed her and took off my jacket and handed to her. I was standing close to her and I could smell her perfume. She could feel me standing behind her, she kept the jacket in the closet and she turned to face me. I could see that she was breathing heavily, and her whole body was shaking with passion.

I pulled her to me and bend down to kiss her. She tip-toed to close the gap and we kissed again, but this time gently and passionately, as if we had all the time in the world and as if we really needed to savour this moment. She tasted headier than the headiest wine I had in my life. I could feel a bit of giddiness as blood rushed into my extremities. Her moaning against my lips and tongue was not really helping this moment. My thirst was all but forgotten.

"I want to make love to you", I said, voicing my real thoughts, "all night, if possible."

"Yes, make love to me", she said, her voice hoarse with passion. Her lips were a deep red now and very inviting. I wanted to kiss her again, but the rational me, who was fast dying in the face of the possibility of sex with a very attractive person, had to ask the question.

"Are we moving too fast?" I ask her in a whisper, my lips brushing against her. Rational me was hanging on by a thread, *Die, you rational bastard, Die!*

"What? Don't fuck with me now. I waited a long time for this… seven years, if we count the time we went for that dinner!" she exclaimed, very seriously, grabbed me and started kissing me hungrily again. With that, the 'rational me' went into a coma. She started dragging me to her bedroom, mumbling, "I hope you are carrying protection". I managed to grab my bag, as I always had extra condoms in my bag's media pocket, other than that I have two in my wallet. When I said "all night long", I meant "all night long", I have been preparing for "all night long" for a long time.

Jade turned on the heater in the room, and I switched my phone from Do Not Disturb mode to Airplane mode this time; I could see that there were more WeChat messages and Whatsapp messages. Those messages can wait if needed forever. We stripped off our layers of clothing and she echoed my frustration about wearing so many layers in the winter. We were finally down to our inners. There was a pile of clothes next to the foot of her queen-sized bed.

Both of us hesitated to take the first step. What if this was not as good as we hoped it would be? After about a minute of eying each other and hesitating, we reached for each other and sat on the bed and started kissing each other again. My restraint was all but gone. I started kissing her all over her body. She was getting more excited and her breathing was getting heavier and heavier.

I tried to remove her brassiere, but she pushed my hand away. I was surprised as my assumption was we were going to go all the way. For a second, I thought there was some misunderstanding and my idea of "making love, all night long" was different from her idea of "making love, all night long".

"You first, I want to see you naked", she whispered hoarsely.

I removed my underwear and except my Fitbit, I was completely naked. I got back on to the bed too, kneeled on the bed and waited for her to do her bit.

"Oh dear, you are very beautiful", she said looking at me. I have never been called attractive in my life and the comment that I am "beautiful" made me blush. Guess all the workout paid off. Despite the dimness in the room and my dusky skin tone the blush showed. She saw the blush and started giggling.

She got out of the bed slowly unclasped her brassiere and removed it sensually. Her skimpy panties followed and she was laid bare before my eyes. She was perfect with the perfect curves and firm body. She had a small scar under her right breast but otherwise, she was flawless. I loved the fact that she had chosen to not to wax or shave her womanhood. I could see that she was getting excited.

My eyes might have lingered too long down there, and she quickly covered her womanhood with the right hand.

"I am sorry, I don't like shaving down there", she said shyly, and added quickly "I can shave if you are turned off by the hair."

I quickly get out the bed, walked to her, removed her hand, looked into her eyes and told her sincerely, "You are perfect and you look beautiful the way you are. I was just lost for words and was thinking how lucky I am to have known you. Don't change one thing!"

I went back and sat on the edge of the bed, slipped on a condom and dragged her close to me. She knew instinctively what I wanted, and she got on top of me. She kissed me passionately and I could feel the heat radiating from her centre. I pull her closer to me and felt her breast pressing against my chest.

One moment we were two different people, the next we became one.

We started hesitantly, touching each other and trying to understand each other's body. We made love gently, passionately, slowly and urgently. Seven years of bottled up passion came bursting out that night. The bedroom was filled with the beautiful sound of our passion. We made love through the night, losing count of how many times we made love. We couldn't get enough of each other, the first three or four time the mere smell and taste of each other were enough for us to start making love again, and we peaked quite fast. We were willing and eager to give each other more.

Later, when one of us thinks we were done, the other would find a way to coax an arousal from the other and make love again. It was a never-ending treasure hunt. We explored each other with our hand, lips, mouth, tongue and our bodies. We lived our imagination to the fullest. Each time we peaked, we did it together and reached higher newer highs we thought was not possible. Finally, when we stopped in the wee hours of the morning, we were fully spent and covered in each-others sweat and saliva. We were not yet satisfied, but we were truly tired, and I had run out of condoms as well.

As we lay there cuddled against each other and gently caressing each other's body, I was sure that I didn't want to be with anyone else. Yes, I was selfish – There was no way I could experience this with anyone else. Everything else and everyone else was a blur, but then I was not sure what Jade's thoughts were about us.

More than once, that night the scary four-letter word – love – came to my mind, but I had pushed it firmly out of my mind as I thought it was a stupid thought to entertain. It was not that I was falling in love with Jade but had fantasized how would it feel to be in love with someone as beautiful as Jade. That fleeting thought came with its own baggage of doubts and questions.

Will it be a jealous love or a generous love? Will I be able to make her happy and take care of her? Will I be able to respect and trust her without any boundaries? Will she accept me for what I am? Was this just a fleeting burst of pent-up passion or something that's real?

I could feel Jade's eyes on me, as I was lost in these thoughts. She was looking at me, but not seeing me. She also seemed to be lost in thought as well.

Chapter 14.   Penny for Your Thoughts

I don't know when I dozed off but when I woke up, we were still in each other's arms, and I realized how thirsty and hungry I felt. She should also be feeling the same.

Jade was lying in my arms with her hands gently caressing my chest. Her eyes were closed and she had a smile of satisfaction on her face. I should ask her if she needed something.

I caressed her shoulder eliciting a gentle moan of satisfaction from her smiling lips, and I asked her, "Do you want something to drink, dar... Jade?"

I bit back the 'darling' that nearly slipped out. If she noticed it, she ignored it.

"Yes dear, I would love some red wine and some water; I think you have seen my wine cabinet. I have few bottles of drinking water on the kitchen counter", she said with her eyes closed, with a smile on her face as she slipped in the 'dear' into her response. Her eyes suddenly flew open, and she added, "Oh... There are some dark chocolate truffles in the fridge, can you us get some? I am starving."

I could do with some unhealthy calories too.

"Lovely, let me go get it for you," I said, jumping out of the bed, ensuring that I don't step into our pile of clothes. I pulled on my underwear and stepped out into the now warm hall. She hadn't turned off the heater in the living room.

The wine glasses were on the coffee table, where Jade had left it. I picked up a Yellow Tail wine, which was a Shiraz reserve and the wine bottle opener. I picked up two bottles of drinking water from the kitchen countertop. I opened the fridge, picked up a box of dark chocolate truffles and headed back into the bedroom, carefully balancing everything in my two arms.

I could make the outline of Jade's body in the bed. She was doing something with her phone. A minute later, soft music filled the air. I saw that she had a JBL Flip on her ornate study table and that's where the music was coming from. She locked and put away the phone. She got out the bed to help me when she saw me precariously balancing all those bottles and chocolates.

She took the water bottles from my arms and kept it one the night table. I placed the wine glasses on the table, opened the wine bottle and poured out two glasses. I opened water bottles and offered one to Jade. We both finished the water in a few seconds, and I realized that she was still naked. I fished out my pullover and my t-shirt from the pile of clothes. I wore my t-shirt and gave the pullover to Jade, who slipped it on and whispered a "thanks".

I sat next to her and offered her one of the wine glasses. We clinked the wine glasses and started drinking the wine. She started peeling the foil off the chocolates and started eating them. I stared at the chocolate like a hungry puppy and started making tiny puppy-like whining noises. She popped a few of them into my mouth, giggling all the while.

I stopped making those noises and finished the wine. I could sense that she was in a pensive mood and I hoped that she was not regretting this. She was still savouring the wine and enjoying the chocolate, so I refilled my glass and started sipping the wine slowly. I moved my wine glass to my left hand and moved close to Jade until our shoulders were touching. She seemed deep in thought and I wanted to be there for her if she wanted to talk.

"Penny for your thoughts?" I asked her as gently as possible.

"Hmm?" she looked up questioningly, her eyes shining in the dark.

"I mean, you have that look. As if there is something you want to get off your mind. I am here if you want to talk Jade" I looked as genuine as I sounded. I put down my wine glass as it was starting to go through my head. I had started craving for some real food also.

She continued to sip the wine in silence until she was done with the wine. I topped up her glass, corked the bottle and place it next to my wine glass. She was taking some time to make up her mind.

She finally looked at me, her eyes shifting between my left and right eye, and said, "I want to tell you something, Anand. I want you to listen with an open mind and I hope you don't judge me. I want you to think about this very seriously and let me know what you think. I know this will sound a bit abrupt, but I have had a lot of time to think about this."

She was very serious and I knew from her face that this was going to be some deep pent-up thought that she has been holding on to for some time.

"I am no one to judge you, Jade, so please tell me whatever you want to tell me", I told her reassuringly with a decisive nod of my head.

She took a sip of the wine, took a deep breath and started talking.

"Anand, you have always been in my heart since we first met seven years back. You have stayed there through all the ups and down in my life. I have more money than I can spend now thanks to my inheritance from my father and I want nothing else in life now, other than… giving us, giving this a shot. I guess, what I'm trying to say is that I like you very much. You were always respectful, committed and had your values, strange as it was for me back then, now it makes sense to me. Despite the stupidity of my youth, you remained respectful to me and were a good friend to me until we drifted apart."

I knew at that point what she wanted, though it should have been obvious to someone with a bit more intelligence when she asked me to be "open minded".

"If it is okay for you, can we try seeing each other for some time? For most parts, you are a reserved person and you tend to hold back your thoughts, so I am asking you this. The chemistry between us is great. In fact, it's more than great, it is fantastic, but I want this to me more than just a physical relationship. I tried to picture you and me together, and that was a good picture. I want us to get to know each other better. I want us to see if we can go beyond a physical relationship only."

I managed to keep a straight face since the thought of us going beyond just a physical relationship had come up quite a few times in the night when we were making love. I liked Jade, and here she is, asking if we can give us a shot at a serious relationship. She was studying my face to try and gauge my reaction and I showed her my thoughtful listening face. She took another sip of the wine and continued.

"If you think that this is workable for us, then I would like us to be in an exclusive relationship."

She paused for a minute to allow that to sink into me. I smiled and nodded. I knew that if I agreed to see Jade, I wouldn't want to think of anyone else. I had remained largely impassive when she was talking, so she emphasized, "I know you need some time to think about this, but I do want you to think about this."

She had no idea how close I was to jump into this, but I needed to think seriously about this. I slowed myself down.

"I am feeling really hungry. Are you hungry, Anand?" she asked me abruptly changing the subject. Perhaps she was worried that I would reject without giving it any thought. Before I could say anything and my stomach made an involuntary rumbling noise in response.

She giggled and pecked me quickly on my lips and said "Let me make some pancakes and coffee for you. You do like pancakes, right?"

"I love pancakes. Let me help you and please don't say no", I told her, trying not to let my emotions show when I spoke.

"I wasn't going to say no. I want your help. No free breakfast. Oh, by the way, if we are trying this, don't expect me to do everything", she stuck her tongue out playfully.

"That thought never crossed my mind", I replied earnestly.

"Good, now let's get dressed and let start cooking. I am starving", she said, pushing me playfully off the bed.

Chapter 15.   Making Pancakes Her Way

We dressed up quickly, and when she removed the pullover to dress up, I was reminded how perfect she was. She blushed a bit under my unabashed stare and it was my turn to giggle.

She wanted to use the bathroom and freshen up a bit. I wanted to use the bathroom as well, but I could wait.

I could see some of the stealth wealth in her kitchen. Her chimneys were imported, so was the kitchen stove. Her utensils, knives and cutlery were all from either Zwilling J.A. Henckels or from some Japanese brands made with hand folded steel. She seemed to use Tupperware for almost all storage. A quick look at the food cabinets and the refrigerator. Most of the food seemed to come from some imported food store or organic foods store.

She came back, looking renewed, and noticed that I was exploring her kitchen. She blushed a bit, and added shyly, "I like to cook, so I spend money on these sort of things".

"I like to cook too, just that right now most of my utensils, knives and cutlery are from Ikea. I will feel a bit embarrassed to invite you home," I said with a smile.

"God! You are an idiot, Anand. I don't care about all these things. You said you are single. Now invite me to your home and cook for me... And you better cook some Indian food for me. No matter where your kitchenware or utensils are from", she said with her hands folded across her chest. She was smiling, but I knew that she was waiting expectantly for a response from me.

"Alright, Alright, I invite you to spend time with me on a weekend. Let me show off my cooking skills to you", I said with a bit of flourish. I really hope that she doesn't end up hating my cooking so much that she will change her mind about us.

"Good! Do you have any nut allergies? I do remember, you are allergic to crustaceans. I want to serve my special pancakes with butter, peanut butter, maple syrup and honey", she inquired as she took out four eggs from the fridge and cracked them one by one into the food processor bowl. She carefully removed two yolks and discarded it down the sink.

"Nope, I am not allergic to anything else", I replied as she added a large pinch of salt and a cup of full cream milk. I was a bit surprised that she still remembered about my crustacean allergy. She's just so amazing and thoughtful. Why am I even thinking so much about giving this relationship a shot? I should man up and just say 'yes'. I also made a mental note to remember what she liked and what she didn't.

She proceeded to add a tablespoon of stevia, half a cup of vanilla whey protein and blended this for two minutes. In another bowl, she mixed one cup of oats flour, half a cup of whole wheat flour, a tablespoon each of flax seeds and chia seeds, one teaspoon baking soda and a quarter teaspoon baking powder. I helped her mix the mixture together until it looked evenly distributed. We slowly blended in the dry mix into the wet mix using the blender itself, until the batter looked creamy enough. Some people say lumps in pancakes are okay, I guess Jade and I didn't share that belief. I quickly washed the bowl and wiped it clean with a paper kitchen towel. Jade poured out the batter into the bowl and using a spatula got out the last bits of the batter into the bowl.

"Does it look a bit thick to you?" she asked after studying the batter for few seconds.

I nodded my agreement and said, "A little, I think you can add a little milk or water".

She added some more milk and stirred in the batter until it had a familiar pancake consistency. While she did this, I found out where she had kept her pan, and I found that she had four kinds of pans. I selected the flat one, rinsed it under the running water and wiped it clean with the kitchen towel. Jade seemed pleased with the choice of the pan and, my compulsion to clean everything. I place it on the kitchen top. I didn't fire up the stove yet, as Jade had covered the bowl with a cling wrap and started a twenty-minute timer to rest the batter.

"Can you help to get the butter from the fridge?" she asked me as she started putting away ingredients. She brought out a box of Nespresso capsules, a Nespresso VertuoLine coffee machine, and a milk steamer from one of the cabinets. She got out two cups, which were white IKEA 365 cups; I recognized the cups as these were the ones I used at my home.

I found the butter in the chill tray and it was some imported brand from New Zealand, called Alpine. I made sure that I got the unsalted one. I placed the butter in the saucer, that Jade had kept next to the batter.

Meanwhile, Jade poured in some milk into the steamer and started it. She selected two Livanto Espresso capsules for herself and I selected two Capriccio coffee capsules for myself.

"How do you like your coffee?" she asked me, which sort of indicated to me that she likes to drink her coffee with milk.

"I like it with very little milk in the morning for the first cup. For my second cup, I take it black. During the day, I like to drink Latte", I said, explaining my preferences.

She made my first cup of coffee for me and added a bit of the steamed milk. She then made a double shot latte for herself.

We stepped out into the apartment balcony to enjoy the coffee with a cigarette. We lit up our respective cigarettes and sipped our coffees, enjoying the warmth of the coffee. I wanted to ask her if she had any other thoughts or if she wanted to know something about these past seven years of my life, or maybe that comes after I have made up my mind. I didn't really care about her past, but if she wanted to tell me something, it's up to her.

"I know you might have questions about the past, but I want to assure you that my past is in the past and there is nothing that will come back to haunt us", she said at the exact moment. I can never understand how most women around me can read my mind so easily. It was possible that I end up meeting people who can easily read my mind.

We both heard the faint 'ding' as the kitchen timer reached the 20-minute mark. Jade and headed back into the kitchen. I turned on the stove and Jade discarded the cling wrap and mixed the batter again. I tried to stifle a yawn, which Jade caught from the corner of her eye.

"Why don't you go and rest a while if you want? I can do this." Jade volunteered.

"I am good. We had a very active night, which is why I am a bit tired", I said with a cheeky smile on my face.

She punched my shoulder playfully and said "You pervert! At least go and freshen up. I have kept out some towels and a spare toothbrush."

She showed me to the bathroom and added, "And... once you come back, don't just stand there staring at me. Help me slice the butter into one-centimetre cubes."

I drained the rest of the coffee before, heading to her bathroom which as extremely utilitarian but was well laid out. I used the toilet and brushed my teeth. My clothes smelled okay, so I stripped down and stood under the cold shower for full two minutes before turning off the faucet. I towelled myself dry, dressed up again, and headed back into the kitchen.

Jade had set the table with a pair plates, cutlery and glasses. She had poured some more milk into the steamer and had taken out four more Espresso capsules. She gave no indication of noticing I had showered. She was stirring the pancake batter and seemed deep in thought. She was probably thinking as to how to tell me whatever she wanted to tell me.

I opened the foil-cover of the butter paper, placed it on a heavy bamboo cutting board, washed the knife in ice-cold water and sliced out a centimetre-thick slice of the butter while ensuring that I don't damage the foil. Rewrapping the butter is a nightmare if you damage the foil. I then proceeded to cut the butter into little one-centimetre cubes and dropped them into the bowl of ice water Jade had prepared for me. I had to do this fast to ensure that the butter didn't melt from the heat of my hands. We had some thirty odd little cubes waiting to be consumed. I rewrapped the butter in the foil and put it back into the fridge. Jade was testing the heat of the pan with a drop of water and she looked satisfied. I washed the knife and the cutting board, wiped them carefully, and returned it to their appropriated placed.

Jade took the bowl with butter in ice water, and carefully dropped a butter cube on to the pan. She spread the butter gently over to the pan using the spatula. Shen then ladled about a third of a cup of batter on to the pan. She had a smile of satisfaction when it spread evenly without much effort to form a nice round pancake. She then dropped a cube of butter on top before the trademark holes started forming. That was new for me, as I never added butter on top.

The delicious smell of the buttery pancake filled the kitchen and I started salivating at the thought of eating a stack of peanut butter and maple syrup. Jade turned on the chimney to avoid the kitchen from getting smoky.

She flipped it at the right time – the holes were starting to form and the top firm enough. The melted butter on top sizzled when it hit the hot pan, sending another burst of butter flavour through the air. She cooked the pancake for 2 minutes more. This was the test preparation.

She slid the pancake off the pan onto a plate and poked it with a toothpick to see if it was cooked inside. The toothpick came out clean and she smiled and whispered "Perfect". She proceeded to make the rest of the pancakes in batches of three, until we a total of twelve little pancakes, four each for us, and four extras in case, we were feeling hungrier. She covered the remaining batter with a cling wrap before keeping the bowl in the fridge.

She made me a black coffee and made herself another double latte. We dug into the pancakes and polished off our pancakes in less than 10 minutes. After a slight hesitation from both of us, the extra pancakes disappeared as well. She had her pancakes with some Manuka honey and butter. I had mine with lots of peanut butter and maple syrup. It was the first time I have had this kind of pancake, and it was surprisingly delicious. This amazing breakfast deserved a smoke.

I think I have the most readable face in the world, as at that exact moment Jade said, "You look like you want a smoke. I could use a cigarette myself."

Chapter 16.   One More Request

We took the coffee to the balcony and light up a cigarette each. I sighed a sigh of satisfaction as the cigarette pushed the oxytocin high from sex and serotonin high from the breakfast, even higher. I could see that Jade was experiencing something similar as her eyes were closed and she had a faint smile of satisfaction on her face.

The sunlight fell on her face and highlighted her features. Now that I have lived in China long enough, it was easier to see the European features in her. The shape of her cheekbones, the nose, the shape and colour of her eyes were so different from your average Chinese. Nicole was certainly beautiful, but except her nose, her features were typical of Chinese. Jade had beautiful features, and when all those features came together, she was pleasing to the eyes but not stunningly beautiful, but still out of my league. My thoughts came back to what Jade had asked me when her voice interrupted my thought.

"In fact, I have another request, if you do want us to try this... relationship. I want us to get tested, as I prefer using birth control pills, rather than condoms. I do like us to have the option of being spontaneous", she added hesitantly.

I can understand her trepidation, as she was not sure of my history. The general perception of foreigners was generally unfavourable and some of us are perceived as a promiscuous bunch. Perhaps she shared the same concern. The way I understood this request is as a way to bury our past should we agree to go forward with this. I am happy to get tested as many times as needed, but I was not sure about not using condoms. I was not ready for unplanned pregnancies. I just don't trust birth control pills. This is probably one point I will have to push back on.

"Understand, I am okay for us to get tested. I am just not sure about not using condoms... birth control pills can be unreliable sometimes", I replied.

What I'd hoped to convey at that moment was that I am seriously thinking about what she asked from us and, also convey that I was not interested in accidental pregnancies at this point of time, however serious we might become.

"And Jade… To be honest, I had the same thought of giving us a try, but I have been thinking about this, uh… more recently than you. I do need some time to think as I don't want to ruin our friendship and what we can have by rushing into this", I added hastily.

"I want you to think about this, very seriously", she replied, stressing on the words 'very seriously', "Like I indicated before, I had a lot of time to think about this. Take as much time as you want to think, but I want you to know that whatever is your decision, I will respect it", she said. Perhaps it was my imagination, but I detected a bit of sadness in her voice when she said that. It was almost as if she was saddened by the thought that I might not agree.

I drew her close to me and gave her a quick hug and kiss. This pacified her and her beautiful smile was back. I wanted to make love to her again then and there, but I held back as the timing was inappropriate and more importantly, I didn't have any condoms left with me.

"Yes, I understand", I said, but not because I understood her completely, but because I had nothing else to say. I am completely useless when I'm sleep deprived and after a night of sex.

We had reached a point where we had nothing more to talk about, so we finished our respective coffees and cigarettes in silence.

"I am going change the passcode today…" she said as we headed back to the apartment, and added with a naughty wink, "I will change it to today's date. It was worth the wait."

"Aww, I'm touched. You shouldn't have told me that, I can just walk in and take advantage of you… Even before I have made up my mind", I said with an impish smile and a wiggle of my eyebrow. *Perhaps not too useless after all,* I said to myself at my attempted wit.

"We will see about who is taking advantage of whom. I am hoping you would make up your mind, then let me know, so that we can take advantage of each other for some time to come", she retorted not willing to be one-upped by a man. We both laughed and stayed away from each other as I could feel that we both wanted to rush into each other's arm make love again.

The attraction was tangible. Did I tell you before, we were like two magnets forcefully separated? Our breaths were shallow and our lips dry as we tried to calm down. Jade's pupils were dilated and I was sure that my eyes were dilated as well. I was itching to throw caution in the wind, but I was saved by the bell, rather my phone's weekend alarm which reminded me it was 8:30 AM in the morning, on Sunday. Workday alarms were set at 5:30, 6:00 and 6:30 in the AM.

We were both equally startled and we both started laughing embarrassingly at the fact we were this close to madness. I took out the phone and killed the alarm.

"Looks like it's time to head back home. I am on leave the next week and will be in Shanghai during the spring festival. We can meet for a lunch or coffee… outside", I suggested and added the 'outside' quickly to ensure that there would be no misunderstanding as to why we are meeting.

"Haha, you don't need to justify everything you say. I understood you perfectly", she said laughing at my blundering efforts to sound politically correct. I could sense she had something else to say, and as expected she continued on, "But, I will be travelling tomorrow to Palermo, Italy with my mother and grandparents from my mother's side to take care of some of the legal aspects for my inheritance from my father, and then a holiday in Europe. We can meet only after I come back, which is a week after the spring festival, or three weeks from now."

I was crestfallen and my face showed it, I was hoping to meet her and get to know a bit more about her. Seeing my dejected expression, she tried to pacify me, "Anand, this is a good thing, as you have will have time for yourself and you can use this opportunity to think objectively about us. If you need to talk we can always talk on WeChat."

"You are right, I do need some time to think objectively about this. I want you to know that I am dying to say yes, but I don't want to hurt you by rushing into this", I replied acknowledging that the three-week separation is the best for us.

Her face lit up with my 'dying to say yes' comment. I drew her into my arms and against my chest and embraced her and she embraced me back with an intensity that showed how much she cared for me. I didn't dare give a name to what I felt and what she might be feeling.

No, I told myself, you need to think really hard about this. For now, let her go.

I gently let her go and could see that her face was tilted upward in expectation of a kiss. Instead, I give her a respectful kiss on her cheeks, smiled and said, "Take care Jade, I need to go now. I will see you in three weeks."

If she was disappointed, she hid it well with a dazzling smile. She nodded in agreement and gave me a hug again. She mumbled something into my chest.

"What? I didn't catch that", I told her as I let her go.

"I said, I am going to miss you a lot", she said, looking up.

"I will miss you too Jade", I replied and that seemed to pacify her. I had already started missing her. I wanted to meet her once more before I go, maybe for dinner. I should ask her right away, and then cancel on Nicole, but unfortunately, I am not that kind of a friend; I don't cancel on my friends.

I knew that I can see Jade on WeChat, but that is not really seeing her. No electronic communication in the world can yet replace this feeling of togetherness, that fact that I could smell her, feel the warmth and affection radiating from her, hear her breathing, her eyes begging me to stay and go at the same time, and her hands on my arms not willing to let me go.

She let go of my hand hesitantly, walked me to the main door and saw me off. As I stepped out, I turned back to see her and she was standing on the pedestal, a lot of expectation written on her face. With Jade watching, I walked down the flight of stairs and when I reached the first landing, I was gripped by an illogical thought.

What if she changes her mind in the coming three weeks? What if she finds someone better in Italy? I turned around to see Jade standing there at the pedestal, with a strange look on her face. It almost looked like fear to me. It was then it hit me - *Did she share the same fear?* I stood there at the first landing, she at the pedestal and we were looking searchingly at each other's face to understand what was going on in each other's minds. I would have given anything to know what was going on in her mind. What exactly did she feel about me?

"Anand, I... I like you very much. I hope you can feel that. I will be thinking of you every second. Please think about this... about us seriously", Jade called out across the gap, and breaking the uneasy silence, almost as if in response to my thought.

"Jade, me too... I mean, I will be thinking about you, about us, every second for the next three weeks. I will see you once you are back", I replied.

We hastily exchanged 'goodbyes' before we did something illogical like rushing into each other's arms again. I started walking down the stairs after Jade hesitantly closed the door.

As I walked down the stairs, a thought hit me hard. I was actually scared to admit how much I liked her at that point, as I was seeing her after such a long time. But, to be perfectly honest, I was even more afraid that I might just be infatuated with her. If I am just infatuated, I would know it in three or four days, the worst case within a week. I have been infatuated and in love before, many times, and I know how that felt, and this felt completely different. I have had a few superficial relationships and I know how that felt – I would wake up in the morning to see the lady gone or I would leave the lady's home without disturbing her; this depends on whose house we were in or which hotel we ended up in.

This didn't feel superficial, and this didn't feel like infatuation, and it was scary feeling not knowing what exactly the relationship was. As I stepped out into the courtyard and started walking toward the general direction of the metro station, I had a strong feeling that this might be a relationship that might lead to something, that went beyond any of those relationships I had in the past, including a failed marriage when I was 27, which was a well-kept secret in the family and a close circle of friends.

This failed marriage had left me unable to think of any long-term relationships and had broken my spirit for a long time. I never expected that a person I knew and loved for 7 years since my college days would leave me in the first week of our marriage... No, not leave... Run away with someone she met a mere six months ago.

Thanks to a clause in the Indian marriage act, and family connections, the marriage was annulled in the next couple of weeks. The shame was too much for me to bear, and I was on the verge of going into depressive mania, but my parents and my friends never gave up on me and eventually helped me recover.

I left India that very year and vowed never to go back to India. In fact, also, I vowed to never fall in love again, which kept me from ever getting too close to anyone. Interestingly, It also made me very empathetic and understanding towards peoples. I was the perfect friend, but never the perfect partner. This was the hidden side of me, Anand the smiling guy who's shy, friendly and polite, but could never hold on or never made an effort to hold on, to a girlfriend for more than a year, other than that one girl I got serious about... serious enough to invest my life savings into an expensive education (which in retrospect was one of the best decisions of my life).

I was close to the metro stop and I decided to put all these thoughts on the back burner, as there is no way I could think normally when I was emotionally charged up and confused. I didn't want to think of my past and my failures. It was time to turn my attention to my phone, which was ignored for so long. I was not sure how the battery lasted so long... *Ah yes, I had put my phone into the Airplane mode.*

I entered the metro stop and stood on the platform waiting for the train to come.

It was time to open the floodgates and let the messages in.

Chapter 17.   An Evening's Worth of Text Messages

I was half-afraid of what would happen when I turn off the Airplane mode and I discovered that my fears were well-founded. The moments I connected to the network, the phone was flooded with about eleven hours' worth of message notifications. Here's what I am going to do, I am going to categorize it by people who sent me the messages rather than the message source (SMS, iMessage, Whatsapp or WeChat).

Parents

They had messaged me inquiring about my health and how come I didn't turn up for the weekly video call on WeChat. We usually have the call at around 9 PM on Saturday evenings, my time.

I texted back and lied to them that 'I was down with a bit of cold', and that 'I had put the phone on Airplane mode' (that bit was true of course), and that 'had gone off to sleep early' (a lie again – I didn't sleep one bit during the night).

Allen Huang

A train heading in my direction had arrived on the platform and I had boarded that train.

If one were to read Allen's message, he or she would feel that Allen was on verge of mental breakdown. There were five text messages, eight WeChat messages and four missed call alerts, all in a space of two hours spanning from around 10 PM to midnight. This is how the messages went.

```
Allen (WeChat): Dude, did you accept
the request from Alice?
```

Allen (WeChat): Dude, I am sorry, don't be pissed off at me.

Missed call alert (Text): You have (two) missed call(s) from Allen Huang

Allen (iMessage): WTF Dude, why are you not answering my calls?

Allen (iMessage): Oh okay, your phone is turned off... Sorry.

Possibly realizing he was using iMessage, switches over to WeChat

Allen (WeChat): Jean said, she just saw the messages Alice sent you. She was upset and apologetic. Jean apologised on behalf of Alice. You know that that is very rare.

Allen (WeChat): What exactly did she say? Jean didn't say anything to me.

Allen (WeChat): Whatever it is, just ignore her okay? You are an awesome guy and deserve better than that crazy lady.

Missed call alert (Text): You have (one) missed call(s) from Allen Huang

Allen (WeChat): Bro, I hope you got lucky and that's why your cell phone is off

Allen (WeChat): When you turn cell back on, I want you to delete Alice's

> messages, and forget anything
> happened.

Half an hour later.

> Allen (WeChat): I hope you are not upset with me.
>
> Missed call alert (Text): You have (one) missed call(s) from Allen Huang
>
> Allen (iMessage): Okay dude, call me when you can. I hope you don't read those messages.

After this there no messages. Since he begged me to not to read Alice's messages, the only obvious thing to do was to read those messages. I replied to Allen.

> Anand Nair (WeChat): Dude I am okay. I didn't read her messages. I will delete it. Sorry, I had turned off my phone. Talk more when we meet.

He responded immediately.

> Allen (WeChat): Okay dude. That's good. Hope you got lucky ;-).

I was not going to take the bait.

Alice Wang

The first message was relatively harmless; obviously, this was not the message Allen was talking about.

> Alice Wang (WeChat): Hi, yes nice to meet you too.

About an hour or so later, during which, she possibly browsed my WeChat moments (a social timeline like that of Facebook), she messaged back.

This is the verbatim of her message, with grammatical errors and all that.

> Alice Wang (WeChat): Hi Anand, Jean and Allen didn't tell me before that you are from Indian. Please don't mind if I say this but I don't date people from Indian and Pakistan.
>
> Alice Wang (WeChat): You all are big cheats, and you country full of rapists. You know, I have to be honest, we Chinese people generally don't like you country people. And I prefer American or European people now. Sorry, I don't think I can go out with someone like you.
>
> Alice Wang (WeChat): Also, I found from Jean that you don't have a car or apartment in China.

Ok... Wow! Even at my age, there is a first time for everything! That was the first time, I have experienced real discrimination in China, at least from people who are of my generation. The comment about car and apartment is a fairly common one, so I was impervious to that comment. Usually, I would have sent back a nasty response and tried to educate her about India but I was still basking in the afterglow of sex and my thoughts were mostly about Jade and how should I respond to Jade's request (you can see that under messages from Jade). And, yes, she actually thought my country is called 'Indian'. So, my response, fully expecting Alice to have blocked me, was simple.

> Anand Nair (WeChat): Ok whatever, good luck finding whatever you want :-).

Surprisingly, the message went through, so I went into her profile and blocked her from seeing my moments and muted her. This is just in case she continues to spy on my moments or she feels the urge messaging me back. In retrospect, I should have blocked her.

The train had reached my stop and I had gotten off the train.

Jean Li

Now that Allen's messages made sense, Jean's rare message was no surprise to me. She had sent and recalled two messages, and the one that finally remained in the chat log was this one.

```
Jean Li (WeChat): Sorry, Anand. I
didn't expect Alice to act this way.
Please don't be upset.
```

Jean might be a hard ass sometimes, but she liked me and trusted me, and today, I really liked the fact that she was willing to lose face in front of me.

```
Anand Nair (WeChat): I didn't read
her messages, Allen asked me not to.
So, I guess I am okay.
```

I can't go and tell Jean a different story and cause confusion. I have learnt long back that, the trick behind lying is consistency. The message and the story have to be consistent, no matter where you tell it, whom you tell it to and when you tell it. Visualize it happened, live that event in your mind and believe it happened. She messaged a few minutes later.

```
Jean Li (WeChat): Oh, that is a
relief. Still, you find out new
things about people you thought you
knew. I am sorry again. Next time we
meet you should sing the whole of
Xiao Pingguo for us :-).
```

Right! As if I will ever sing a Chinese song ever again in my life! I thought when I tapped out the response.

>   Anand Nair (WeChat): Sure, looking
>   forward to it.

Nicole Zhang

I was less nervous about reading Nicole's messages now that I knew where Nicole stood in my perspective.

The first couple of messages was sent at around 12 PM on Saturday when I was asleep.

>   Nicole Zhang (WeChat): Hi, Anand,
>   thanks for your help. Really do
>   appreciate it. I hope you don't get
>   the wrong message from the way I
>   behaved. Even though we just met, I
>   would like to think of you as my
>   friend.

Nope... I am happy to stay in the friend zone. In fact, now that things might get serious with Jade, more than happy.

>   Nicole Zhang (WeChat): I look forward
>   to meeting tomorrow for dinner.

The next message was sent at about 10:00 PM on Saturday.

>   Nicole Zhang (WeChat): Hi, Anand, I
>   am sorry, something came up for
>   tomorrow evening. We will have to
>   meet some other time. Monday or
>   Tuesday okay for you? We can meet by
>   6:00 PM on either of these days.
>   Let's meet there directly. Very sorry
>   again.

A huge wave of relief hit me as I read this message. I don't have to cancel on Nicole. This actually was a great news

> Anand Nair (WeChat): Hi Nicole, no
> problems at all. Let's try to meet on
> Monday at Blue Frog. They have offers
> on burgers and a nice happy hour. PS:
> I consider you as a friend as well :-
>).

Nicole messaged back when I was about to message Jade and ask her out for dinner.

> Nicole Zhang (WeChat): Good :-), See
> you on Monday.

I was halfway back home at this point in time.

Jade Lin

Now that I am not meeting Nicole, I wanted to message Jade and ask her out for dinner on Sunday, as she was leaving on Monday, but Jade had messaged me twenty or so minutes back.

> Jade Lin (WeChat): I am going to miss
> you so much, my dear Anand. I now
> hate the fact I am going away for
> three weeks. Do you think we can meet
> today evening?
>
> Jade Lin (WeChat): I miss you, Anand.
> I am not saying this to force a
> decision. Take as much time as you
> want, but I genuinely miss being with
> you. I wish you had stayed back for
> some more time.

I realized that I was missing her too and quite suddenly the fear of losing her gripped me again and immediately realized that such fears were unfounded. In less than half-an-hour, Jade had started missing me, and I could feel deep inside me that whatever we shared was meant to go on for a long time.

> Anand Nair (WeChat): I miss you too darling. Since you are leaving tomorrow, may I invite you for a drink and dinner today evening at TGI Friday's by the Bund?

I hit sent and waited for her response with my fingers crossed. I was nearly home. I should be feeling sleepy, but I was feeling quite okay. I couldn't stop thinking about her.

> Jade Lin (WeChat): Absolutely, I would love that. Shall we meet at Lujiazui Station, Exit 2 by 5:00 PM?

Something inside me leapt with joy and I let out a shot whoop of joy. People actually stopped to stare at me. I grinned like an idiot and continued walking.

> Anand Nair (WeChat): Sounds like a date.

> Jade Lin (WeChat): Yes, it is. You better be there on time. ;-)

I don't think I will be late. On the contrary, I will be there twenty minutes early.

> Anand Nair (WeChat): Of course, darling. Now go sleep.

> Jade Lin (WeChat): Okay, I will. You get some sleep. Have you reached home?

> Anand Nair (WeChat): I am about two minutes away. I am just entering my community.

I reached home about two minutes later and turned on the heater in my room. I stripped off my clothes and underwear and dumped them into the laundry basket. I stood under a cold shower and scrubbed myself clean. I towelled myself dry and changed into my sleeping gear and got into the bed. I took out the phone to find one more message from Jade.

```
Jade Lin (WeChat): I am in bed now.
The bed smells of you. God, I miss
you.

Anand Nair (WeChat): I am in bed, but
I wish I was with you now.

Jade Lin (WeChat): :-) I wish the
same too. Go sleep now. Good night
XOXOXOXO.

Anand Nair (WeChat): Good night,
XOXOXOXO, I miss you.
```

With that, I put my phone into Do Not Disturb mode. I also set an alarm for 3:00 PM and 3:30 PM. I then covered my eyes with my eye mask and went to sleep. I was out in less than ten minutes.

Chapter 18.   Something Like A Dinner Date

I woke up with a start as my 3:00 PM alarm blared. My heart was pounding hard, and that usually meant I had a nightmare (or a 'daymare' in this case). I ignored the alarm and took a few breaths to calm myself down. I removed the eye mask, silenced the alarm and got out of the bed, hesitantly. My heart was still pounding away as I walked to the kitchen to make my coffee. I tried to recall what the dream was about but couldn't recall even the tiniest of the details. I gave up with a sigh, switched off the 3:30 PM alarm in advance and prepared my first coffee for the day.

With my coffee in my hand, I headed out to the balcony for a smoke before I headed to the toilet. For some reason, I really couldn't enjoy my smoke, I found it disgusting. I put out the cigarette after just a couple of puffs and finished my coffee as quickly as possible without burning my throat. I should have known that things are changing for me from that one incident, not finishing a cigarette while not sick.

I headed to the bathroom to finish my daily ablutions. The dream still bothered me but I firmly pushed it out of my mind by thinking about Jade and what she had proposed.

The memory of time spent with her came rushing back to me and I felt warm all over. The 'sceptical me' and my head immediately tried to shoot it down as hormones and pheromones. The 'believer me' and my heart told me it was meant to go further if I can let go of the past and accept the now without worrying about future... Definitely, need to think hard about this.

I finished my usual cold shower and went to the bedroom to dress up for the evening. I thought for about five minutes what I should be wearing, before giving up and deciding to go with the jeans-shirt-sweater combo. That's as formal as it gets for me. I spend more time applying some hair products and setting my hair to look passably presentable. The improvement was at best, marginal. No hair product could fix my face.

I picked up my sports jacket from my closet and slipped two condoms into the inner pocket of the jacket, in case something was to happen in the night. Better to be prepared than regret later. I took out my hush puppies from the shoe cabinet and slipped it on. It was nearly 4:00 pm by the time I was done with a routine that usually takes me 30 to 35 minutes. This should have been the second indication that something was not quite the same, but this also somehow failed to register.

I unlocked my phone, turned off Do Not Disturb to check if Jade has cancelled on me, and strangely there was only one WeChat message from Jade, at around 2:00 PM reminding me not to be late and lot of hugs and kisses. The other messages were from my parents on WhatsApp, asking me to come on for a video 'after lunch', which is anywhere between 4:00 PM to 5:00 PM my time. If I left by 4:25 I can make it before 5:00 PM to Lujiazui station. Not exactly twenty minutes early, but not late as well.

I started the video call with my parents in WeChat, and the first thing my mother and father noticed was how well my hair was set and "how handsome I looked". I just brushed off the comment as parental affection. After all, to normal parents, their offspring is the most beautiful thing that is there.

As usual, my mother, or Amma as I called her, wanted to talk about every relative in Bangalore. My Father, or Achan as I called him, gave me a financial report of incomes and expenditures. I have told him several times that he need not tell me how they use the money I gave them. His finance and accounting background meant that there was no way he was going to stop until I reach financial "maturity". He was also doing an analysis of portfolio that can give the best returns, and he felt that he found the right portfolio mix for me to invest in, and he decided to stay away from cryptocurrencies. I agreed to transfer over a part of my savings to him so that he can try out that portfolio.

They then dived into the question they usually ask to signal that the call can be concluded– "Did you have someone in your life? Can we start looking for a girl if you are single?"

I gave them the same response I have been giving for past few years – "You will know as soon as I know and please don't look for anyone", but seeing the hopeful look on their faces, I added, "Okay... Don't get too excited, but, I am going to meet someone for dinner, let's leave it at that for the time being."

Both Amma and Achan looked like they were going to burst with joy and break into a Bollywood dance number, as I never mentioned about any girl in the past few years. I have not seen them this happy, since forever. They were this happy when my sister gave birth to my niece, five years back. I was gripped by the fear of letting them down again.

"Amma, Acha, just to be clear. It is just a dinner, don't get too excited", I explained hastily.

"We understand *mone* (son), we don't mind if the girl is Chinese. We just want you to be happy", they replied, already planning for the wedding in their heads, I could see it in their eyes. *What have I done? Damn! I should not have told them anything. Idiot! Idiot!*

"Okay, I got to go now. I am getting late. I love you both" I concluded.

"We love you and miss you *mone*", they said in unison before disconnecting the call.

It was time for me to leave, but instead of walking to a metro stop, I took a Mobike that was illegally parked in the community. I was at the metro stop in less than five minutes, thanks to some crazy biking.

The train towards Lujiazui was neither crowded nor empty, but I saw a drunk guy vomiting in the corner. As I made way to the next car, the comment from Alice about me not owning a car somehow came back to me, and I realized that I should be thinking of getting a car, especially if I am going to be serious about Jade. We can travel to nearby cities in the weekend or just got for long drives when we are bored. Though getting a Shanghai licence plate was next to impossible, I have friends who can help me to get licence plates from nearby cities like, Suzhou or Nanjing. This would allow us to drive around in Pudong where I worked and take weekend trips to nearby cities.

The company I worked for offered interest-free loans for up to thirty-six months and a monthly pretax allowance of RMB 1200. That is, if I buy the car from company's automotive partner, for some models, the company offered assistance of up to 17% for certain small and midsized models. I already started thinking about some of the models that would be suitable for a long drive which was available in the hybrid version too. I had already converted my Indian driving licence to Chinese licence a few months back, so I was covered from that point. I should probably check with the HR or Finance the process of buying the car and applying for the loan. The fact that I was planning my future should have been the biggest indicator that my life had changed forever.

The train reached the Lujiazui station, and I got off the train and turned right to get on to the escalator. I saw Jade facing me with her lips parted in surprise. She was on the same train but two cars in front of mine, so she had to turn left to get on to the escalator, and that when we saw each other. That instant, everything else disappeared and I could only see Jade. Like two powerful magnets drawn to each other, we started walking towards each other, quite unconscious of our surrounding. We were back in our parallel universe, where only two of us existed. One moment we were separated, the next moment Jade was throwing herself into my arms, and the next moment, we were kissing each other. If I were to place an exact time where I knew, that it was going to be difficult to separate us, it was that moment on the platform, although I didn't want to admit this. It was just like being in a movie.

Thankfully, sanity prevailed and we left the metro station, hand in hand. We exited the metro station and used the circular footbridge to cross over to the mall, behind which was located the TGI Friday's. The walk was a pleasant one, despite the fact that the overbridge had more than its share of tourists trying to take photos with the Oriental Pearl Tower in the background.

As we were walking by the mall towards the restaurant, I realized I had forgotten to book tables there, but I was confident that being Sunday, we shouldn't have any issues finding a table.

"I have booked a table", Jade said reading my mind.

"Don't do that! That's so creepy. Am I so readable?" I asked acting dejected.

"Yes, my dear Anand, you are very readable", she said laughing.

"Then my darling Jade... Why are you not reading the fact that I want to make love to you right now?" I asked with a raised eyebrow and a smirk on my face.

"I read it alright, you pervert. I want you to earn it tonight", she said with a wink.

"Ah, so it's going to be like that. Let's see who needs to earn what my darling", I said returning the wink.

She smiled a secretive smile that conveyed more than any words she could have said. It was more than just sexual attraction I felt from her; it felt like she genuinely liked me and I have to admit that this exactly how I felt about Jade... Sometimes you just know it. After a long time, it felt like the universe had given me someone I could trust. My heart skipped a beat at that thought, and as we walked hand in hand, I decided that I want to give it a shot, to hell with thinking for three weeks, but I was still not sure if this is just an infatuation driven by my desire for her or if I genuinely liked her.

I looked at Jade walking beside me, looking thoughtful. What was she thinking? Was she having second thoughts? She didn't look conflicted, she just looked thoughtful.

"Anand," she said, "I want you to know that what happened yesterday means a lot to me and I really didn't do it to force a decision from you. I wanted it to happen because I like you a lot and want to know how it would feel. No matter what you decide, nothing will change what I feel for you."

She had stopped walking and so had I. I could see the earnestness and fear in her eyes. I was overcome with this huge sense of empathy and for a second, then and there, I thought I understand what she felt.

"Jade, I understand what you are trying to say. I like you so much that I fear that...", I blurted out and I just about managed to stop myself from saying "I fear that I'm falling in love with you" and instead finish by telling "...I fear that... this could just be an infatuation and I might end up hurting you. I have always liked you. This three weeks will help me understand how much of this is desire and how much of it is true affection for you. I want you to know this, I have this huge yearning to tell you that I want to give us a shot, but I don't want to fuck things up."

This came out fast and Jade seemed surprised at my display of emotions. I could see the surprise turn to happiness and she expressed that happiness with a quick kiss on my cheeks.

We continued walking hand in hand towards TGI Fridays. I had a smile on my face as I was happy to get my thoughts out of my system. I can enjoy my dinner in peace. I wanted to know how Jade felt and looked at her and saw that she had a placid smile on her face, which told me volumes of how she felt in that moment.

It has been a long time since I have lived in the moment. I had spent most of my time worrying about future or regretting my past. When I was with Jade, I lived in the moment and never thought about the future. Of course, when I am not with her, I did fantasize about a future, but it was focussed on the good things and was not driven by fears or regrets.

We reached TGI Friday's and waited to be seated. It took the restaurant manager a couple of minutes to locate Jade's reservation. As we waited, my phone buzzed a couple of times reminding me, that I had to put my phone on Do Not Disturb.

I took out the phone and saw that it was a WeChat message was from Nicole. From what I could see on the preview on the screen, that she had an emergency, that she wanted to change the time for our meeting and that she would let me know when she can meet, at a later time.

I felt a bit let down for a second, but I was too happy at that point to even reply to the message. I put the phone into Do Not Disturb mode and put it back into my pocket. *I can deal with this later.*

We were seated at a table away from the door and away from the bar, an ideal spot for us to talk. TGI Friday's in Shanghai generally is the ideal quiet spot for people to have a quiet dinner or a quiet drink. We probably got the quietest spot there. As I took off my jacket I noticed what Jade was wearing.

Jade was dressed in a simple white silk blouse and a pair of woollen jeans. The jacket she was wearing was the same from the previous day. She had a simple make up of lipstick, a bit of blush and eye-liner. She looked fabulous. She had gracefully removed her jacket and I noticed that the first button of her blouse was open. I could see a chain with a heart-shaped pendant through the open blouse resting on her chest. She folded her jacket and placed it next to her handbag. I placed the jacket on the back of my chair.

We both sat down and I could clearly see the smooth cleavage of her ample breasts. The night came rushing back again and I was reminded of the feeling of her skin upon my skin, the night before. Before my imagination started running wild, a waitress got us the food menu and drinks menu and left us to decide what we will have for the dinner. She cheerfully introduced herself and reminded us that the happy hour is on until 8:00 PM and all drinks except for wines were on a buy-one-get-one deal.

I waited for Jade to order. She was studying the menu with great interest, which sort of meant that she was probably not used to the menu, which in turn meant she did not come here too often... Or, she was trying to be polite.

"Hmm..." she said while perusing the drinks section of the menu, "I think I will have a mojito today. What about you?"

"I think I will have the Bloody Mary", I replied. I wanted something different, now that my life is taking a turn at this point.

"That's quite a deviation from the gin martini", she said cheekily with a wink.

"Well, since you are willing to be adventurous and go with the mojito, I should try something different, right?" I replied without missing a beat.

She found my response funny and we shared a moment of laughter, before turning our attention to the food menu.

She SHOULD really like me to laugh for that one, I thought.

We debated what would be a good starter and finally settled for a three in one platter and dish of baked potato skins. She wanted the chicken pasta and I decided that a medium done cheeseburger minus the onions and tomatoes, with a side of fries, looked good. We placed the order with a passing waitress and requested for two glasses of water while we waited. The waiter returned with two glasses of water and left to take care of other customers.

Jade's phone vibrated and she glanced down at it. I couldn't read her expression, but she was smiling. She picked it up, typed out a quick message and locked it.

"Sorry, it was something I was expecting for some time now. I needed to respond to that", she said apologetically and quickly added, "It's on 'Do Not Disturb' now."

"It's okay, we live in a hyper-connected world, and that comes with its own advantages and disadvantages", I dismissed her apology with a wave of my hand.

"I know, I have already muted my Facebook and Instagram notifications and I still get far too many notifications... Stuff I just can't turn off", she said in agreement. She had a distant look on her face as if she was trying to remember what all apps she had in her life.

"Yeah, I have turned off notification for Facebook, Messenger and Instagram and still... I get enough to disrupt my normal life. I am on 'Do Not Disturb' during my work hours" I said, sharing her frustration.

We spent the next five minutes complaining about how our lives have been disrupted from being always connected. We ended the conversation by connecting with each other on Facebook and Instagram. The drink arrived right about then.

Other than the fact that celery stalk in Bloody Mary was replaced with two long pieces of sliced celery, the drink was perfect. Jade's mojito looked okay from my angle. We clinked our glasses and took the first sip of our drinks.

"So, tell me a little bit about Palermo. I have read a bit about it on the internet, but I have not really travelled around Europe", I inquired as put down the glass.

"I guess I know as much about Palermo as you do", she said putting down the glass.

I guess the surprise on my face was apparent, so Jade continued, "I was there in Italy when I was really young. This was before my parents separated and got divorced, and my mother came back to China. I only remember the chapels and cathedrals... and the sea". Clearly, she was trying to remember details from over 25 years ago, and she didn't look too happy with those memories.

"Sorry, I... I didn't mean to bring up those memories", I stammered apologetically.

She stared at me for what felt like an eternity before saying, "It is okay Anand. You know very little about my past". She paused to stir the drink and take a sip from it, and added, "Let the past be the past. I should look forward to my future."

I felt something squeezing my heart when she said 'my future' rather than 'our future'. Yes… I understood the stupidity behind hoping for something serious just because we had sex, but to me, it meant something more and I was hoping it meant more to her. I took a sip of the drink to push the thought out of my head; after all the ball is in my court and I have not really said 'yes' to her proposal.

"Hey Anand, don't think about this. So, tell me… How are your parents doing now? And how's your sister and brother doing?" she asked breaking my thoughts and bring me back to reality.

The squeeze on my heart was back at the mention of my brother and this time it was clear on my face. In fact, my eyes misted up and it was hard to hide my flaring nostrils. *Fuck! That hurts.* I tried to recover, but I was a little too slow. There is only so much you can pretend sometimes and I was not sure if I wanted to express my emotions in front of Jade.

"What happened, Anand? Are you okay?" she asked, surprised at my reaction. When I didn't say anything, she added softly, "Listen, whatever it is, I am sorry. Let us not talk about it."

I realized abruptly that I cannot always say I don't want to talk about something just because I don't like it. Perhaps it might be okay to be open for a change and see what happens. I took a large sip of the drink and cleared my throat before I could start speaking.

"No, it is okay", I said putting down the drink, "You had no way of knowing…" My voice cracked a bit and I had to clear my throat again and take another large sip of the drink.

She waited patiently as I collected myself.

"You had no way of knowing that… my brother passed away five years back, in an accident", My voice was cracking again, and I hated myself for being so emotional.

I could hear Jade breathe in sharply at my response. She looked shocked and her face had a look of horror all over it. Her eyes started brimming with tears and her cheeks had flushed red. She was clearly moved. She reached across the table and placed her left hand on my right hand, before whispering hoarsely, "Anand, I had no idea. I am so sorry for your loss. You should have told me when this happened."

"I should have told you, but we were no longer in touch and quite honestly, I haven't told many people about it. It is still a very painful thing for me, and my family", I said fighting back my own tears and swallowing the huge lump in my throat. Jade made no effort to stop the tears that were flowing freely over her flushed cheeks. She was leaning across the table, holding my hands and was weeping quietly.

I was not sure how much I should tell her, but since she was crying, and I was on the verge of crying myself, I decided that things couldn't get any worse. I explained what had happened to my younger brother and how we lost him in a motorbike accident in Bangalore when he was just twenty-five years old. She still had tears rolling down her face at end of my account and I didn't want to stop her.

Usually, I would be conscious of my surroundings and would have tried to console her, so that she would stop crying and so that I wouldn't be embarrassed. In this case, I didn't care. She had lifted my hand and kissed it gently as the tears continued to flow from her eyes. After about a minute or so, I grabbed a napkin and starting dabbing off the tears off her cheeks.

After a few seconds, she gently let go of my hand and took the napkin from my hand, whispered an apology and quickly wiped off the tears. She took a few breaths and regained control of herself. I didn't like her being sad and I didn't want her to leave to Italy this way. I myself took a few deep breaths and regained control over myself.

Jade was looking at me and it looked like she wanted to say something, but at that moment the waiter arrived with our starter platters. He served us and left us. If he noticed that Jade was crying and my eyes were moist, he simply ignored it. I had sort of lost my appetite, and by the way, Jade ignored the food, it looked like she was not too hungry as well. Not even the delicious smell of potato skins or the sight of molten cheese helped.

We continued to sip our drinks quietly and soon the food arrived. The sight of our food failed to reignite the appetite. This date was an unmitigated disaster by all accounts and I was not really doing anything to change it. Our drinks were nearly done and I decided to wait before ordering our next round of drinks.

"This date is not going well", I said with an exaggerated sigh in an attempt to lighten the mood.

"Nothing could be further from the truth. You don't have to assume that a date is all about happy discussion. In fact, I feel closer to you, as you were willing to talk about something that is clearly painful to you and you trusted me enough to share this with me", she said, sounding very surprised and very genuine.

"Really!" it was my turn to be surprised, "I thought I had fucked it up."

"Anand, you are a strange guy. You think that I will judge you for every small thing that happened. How superficial do you think I am", she said chiding me.

"Sorry, I can be an idiot sometimes", I said apologetically trying hard to hide my embarrassment.

She smiled at my comment and said cheekily with a pout on her face, "God, Anand, let's agree not talk about our pasts anymore... At least not now. Can we please start eating or are you going to make me earn my food as well?"

We both laughed at her reference to our earlier conversation on our way to the restaurant. So, despite the fact that we had a rocky start, I felt that we were back on track. We started eating our food. I helped myself to the potato skins and some fried chicken from the platter, and like that, I felt my appetite coming back. By the way, Jade dug into her pasta, her appetite was back too.

Lesson learnt – A delicious meal can sometimes cure the most severe of heartaches, for everything else, you have mindless sex.

We ordered our next round of drinks and politely ignored the waitress' reminder to order more drinks before the happy hour ended, as Jade had to fly next day. That reminded me that I didn't know when she was flying out of Shanghai.

"Is it safe to ask you, what time is your flight tomorrow?" I asked half tongue-in-cheek and half serious; you never know what might trigger off another incident or a bad memory.

She put down her fork with a look of shock on her face and a few moments later, started laughing. I sort of felt stupid and happy at the same time; stupid because I was being too careful, and happy because her whole face had light up and that moment, she looked happy and carefree.

"You are so cute, Anand", she said after she recovered. "Of course, it's okay to ask me what time my flight is. I am flying out at 10 AM from Pudong Airport. I will go back to my grandparents' house tonight and I will leave with my grandparents and mom in the morning. All my stuff is already there."

The first thought that came to my mind was, *So, no sex tonight.* I immediately felt guilty that this was the first thought that came to my mind. I had to redeem myself.

I looked at my watch as if to confirm the time and said, "That's early. We should try and finish up as early as possible so that you can get some rest before flying out tomorrow."

A smile played on her lips when I said this, and she responded with a slight nod of her head. Well, that's that then.

She continued to eat her pasta and helped herself to some fries from my plate, without asking me of course. The burger was fabulous and by the second bite, my appetite was completely back. Jade seemed to like the pasta as well. I had forgotten to ask her where her grandparents' house was, but I had a faint memory that it was in Pudong itself close to where she was living now.

We didn't speak much during the time we ate, and then it hit me that for women to be with someone like me, they need to be very understanding. Except for the occasional flashes of creativity, I am the most boring person out there and I never made an effort to change that. Just not that social or sociable, in my own honest opinion. I am not well travelled enough that I can talk about places or cuisines authoritatively. Except for my own line of work, or few things that interest me, I didn't really care about other's work or life. For example, I honestly had very little idea what a financial controller was and didn't make an effort to understand it for understanding Jade better.

I was suddenly gripped by this fear that I might not go far with Jade and I broke into a cold sweat, which Jade noticed.

"You suddenly look all sweaty and ill at ease. Is everything okay?" she asked me, as I made a mental note to do some research and understand what a financial controller is.

"Oh... I'm good. I just think what a financial controller does and remembered how badly I sucked in Accounting and Finance during my MBA. Just the thought of Accounting and Finance courses scared the living crap out of me", I lied with a smiling face. It's true... I sucked at Accounting and finance so bad that when I got a B+, I actually celebrated with my friends. This believable lie, which was also a fun fact, elicited another laugher from Jade.

I said earlier that she looked pleasing to the eyes, but now I stand corrected, she actually looked stunningly beautiful. Her eyes were shining with delight and I almost fell in love with her.

"I like it very, very much when you smile and laugh", I said as her laughter subsided.

"I love it that you make me laugh", she said with a smile playing on her lips. My heart skipped a beat at the mention of the word "love". The way she smiled really did not help with what I was feeling for her.

We drank to that and quietly continued with our dinner.

Jade finally, finished her dinner first and pushed the plate. I had decimated the burger in about ten minutes and was nibbling on the fries trying to keep her company, so I was relieved when she finally finished her dinner. I was truly full and I couldn't eat another bite. We still had a lot of food left over.

We both looked at the remaining food and at each other and instantly knew that we were thinking the same thing.

"Doggy bag", we both said at the same time and laughed.

We called the waitress and asked her for the check and to package or *da bao* the remaining food. Jade insisted that she should pay the bill, as I had high-jacked the bill for the drinks last night (or early morning depending on how one looked at it). We haggled around for ten minutes as to who should pay for the dinner, the waitress patiently waited with the POS machine in her hand. I grudgingly allowed Jade to make the payment as she showed no sign of relenting and it was close to 8:00 PM now and we still had to finish our drinks. Looks like the condoms in my jacket pocket will remain unused, and that was good in this case.

As Jade made payment using Alipay, the realization hit me that I should be trying to form some good memories with her instead of trying to get her into bed. Any emotional connection that we will form now will go further than any physical relationship we may share at this point in time. Love and lust tend to be temporary, and once all that is exhausted, what remains in the relationship is trust and respect. This was something I have learnt the hard way. If I were to have a relationship with Jade, I need to accept the reality that I am indeed starting this relationship on the basis of lust. Jade seemed to trust me, and that's perhaps the reason why she was willing to have a relationship with me. I should try to repay in kind. As much as I may miss her and wanted her, I needed her to remember me as a gentleman who respects her for the person she is and as someone who can be trusted.

"Jade, let us finish our drinks, and get out of here. I want to take you to the bund", I said as the waitress left us.

This perhaps caught her off guard, as she seemed surprised. She was possibly expecting me to be thinking of ways to get her to sleep with me.

"You see, you need to fly out tomorrow and I was thinking that... you should get proper rest before flying out", I paused to take a drink and added, "Let's take a walk on the bund and then let me drop you back home."

"You do the most unexpected things, Anand. I would love to take a walk with you and I would love it if you can drop me back home", she said with a thoughtful and slightly surprised smile. I could see the admiration in her eyes and perhaps some love. She would have been assuming all along that I was doing everything possible to get her into bed, but then here I was holding back the most primal of instincts and showing her that I cared for her as a person.

Intimacy is a tricky subject and in this materialistic, score keeping, book balancing world we live in, there is a tendency amongst some to believe that every action is a selfish act done to get something in return. It could be a gift, a conversation over dinner or drink, or, a romp in the bed. Intimacy becomes deal based and transactional; you end up keeping account of your actions and what you got in return. You make a note of the size and generosity of the transaction and ensure that you do everything to ensure that you are not in a debt – from the point of, either the size of the gift or the generosity of the action.

For Jade, I was done keeping the book, here is a person for whom I really didn't want to do that.

"I am done with my drink, I am ready to leave when you are", I said pushing away the glass.

"I am done too. Let's go", she said.

She got up, put on her jacket and picked up her purse. I got up, put on my jacket and said, "Let's go."

Jade walked to my side and linked her arms with mine and we walked out of the restaurant. As usual, one of the waitresses thanked us for our patronage on our way out.

We walked up to the promenade and started strolling along the bund. It was a clear, chilly night and we could see the beautiful lights on the west side of the river or the older Shanghai. Pudong might be all new and fancy, but if one truly wants to experience Shanghai he or she should live in Puxi. You will get to enjoy all the aspects, good and bad, of Shanghai life. We could also see a few cruise ships make its way up the river and few barges going up and down the river. There was a light breeze blowing over the river and it ruffled the surface of the Huangpu River giving the reflections on the river a life its own.

"It's really beautiful here", said Jade voicing my thought. I nodded my head in agreement and we continued our walk. We occasionally stole glances at each other and now we were holding hands with fingers intertwined. A sudden gust of wind ruffled Jade's hair and I could see that she was feeling cold. I removed my jacket and draped it over her shoulders.

As I draped the jacket over her shoulders, our eyes locked for a moment and we could see how much we desired each other. I leaned in and kissed her on her lips. The moment our lips touches Jade's arms were around me. I pulled her closer into my arms and kissed her deeply. We were unaware of what was happening around us and we didn't really care. We finally broke the kiss and stood there holding each other tightly.

"Yes", I said.

"What?" she sounded confused.

"Yes, I want to give us a shot. Jade, my darling, I like you so much that I don't want to wait three weeks", I said clarifying what I meant. I was surprised that I found the courage to say out loud what I was thinking.

"Anand, what did you just say?" Jade asked me breathlessly in a small voice.

There were so many emotions on her face and in her voice, that I was afraid that I might have fucked it up. Since I might have fucked it up I repeated, "I said 'I want to give us a shot'".

"Anand, are you sure? Because I cannot stand a heartbreak when it comes to you. So, again, are you sure? Do you want some more time to decide where we need to go from here?" she asked me, her eyes wide and voice slightly breathless. She was still holding on to me and she was pressed against me, her whole body tensed up like a piano wire. Our face was less than an inch apart and I could see her eyes searching my face trying to read me.

"Yes darling, I want us to be together. I like everything about you and I am sure that I want to give our relationship a shot", I said with a smile on my face.

I could see tears of joy filling up in her eyes as she hugged me close and whispered what sounded like, "Thank you". I cradled her head against my chest and kissed her hair.

We stood there holding each other and my heart was filled with joy. I knew that I was going to be very happy with Jade and I wanted to make her happy. We finally let go of each other.

"You just made me very happy Anand", she said in a voice trembling with emotion.

I kissed her gently on her lips and said, "I am happy that I could make you happy. I have always liked you, Jade. I wanted you to know this before you left to Italy."

We hugged again briefly, before resuming our walk. We walked hand in hand, with Jade leaning on my shoulders, until the end of the promenade. We stood by the huge anchor, soaking in the view on the other side and when I looked at Jade, she had a smile on her face and she looked joyous.

She suddenly turned to me and said, "Please don't change your mind. Please wait for me to come back."

"I will not change my mind and I am already wishing that these three weeks goes by quickly", I said in an assuring and assertive tone.

"Can we take a photo together? I don't want to miss you when I'm in Italy", Jade explained.

While I detest having my photo taken, I couldn't refuse her. She took out her phone, open the camera app and put it in selfie mode. She drew closer to me and with the Puxi side of the bund in the background, took five or six photos with various expressions. The final one was of us kissing.

She broke the kiss and said, "Let's go back home, you should be freezing."

We started walking back to the beginning of the promenade. She wanted to give me back my jacket, but I refused as I could see that she was cold. My tolerance for cold was better when I am with beautiful women. I made a mental note to ask her to airdrop photos to me when we are on our way back home.

As we reached the intersection of Fucheng road and West Lujiazui road, I took out my phone and opened the Didi app to order a ride for us (of course I ignored the message that was now piled up in the notification tray), when I realized that I didn't know where exactly Jade's grandparents' house was. I asked her for the address to which she responded by taking the phone from me and typed out the address into the search box. I took the phone back and tapped the ride request button. I had remembered correctly as the house was indeed close to where Jade lived and was one of those newer high-rise apartments. If my memory served me right, those apartments were upwards of twenty million RMB and that realization reflected on my face.

"I used some of my inheritance and bought one of the smaller apartments there for my mother", she admitted hesitantly seeing the expression on my face. She was blushing in embarrassment.

"I see", I said not knowing what else to say. On one hand I was happy that Jade has not changed much since she inherited the wealth from her father, but on the other hand, my insecurities were rearing their ugly heads.

I tapped the 'ride hail' button as I tried to push my insecurities out of my mind. She knows about my family background and she knew that I came from an Indian middle-class family. This was a non-factor for her, as I know that she was also interested in me as a person. This thought made me smile and my smile made Jade smile in relief.

A driver accepted my ride and he called to confirm my location. As we waited for the ride at the intersection, I lit up a cigarette and offered it to Jade. She took it with a smile and started smoking. I lit another one and inhaled on it. It didn't feel disgusting; I guess until I talked to Jade and got my thoughts out, I just didn't feel good about things I usually to do. We quietly enjoyed the smoke in each other's presence and to me, it was as good as the smoke we shared after having the pancakes Jade made for me.

I used this opportunity to ask Jade to airdrop the photos to me. She seemed to know what airdrop was, as she asked me to turn on the Bluetooth and Wifi on phone, which I did then and there. She selected all the photos we took together and shared it with my phone. I saved the photos on to my phone and couldn't help but flip through the photos we had taken together.

The ride arrived about five minutes later and we stubbed out the cigarettes and got into the car. I got in with Jade and closed the door which I had held open for her. The driver confirmed the ride start and we set off towards Jade's apartment. I requested the driver to drop me back home after dropping Jade back home, and he agreed to my request readily.

We sat close to each other and Jade leaned on my shoulder with eyes closed. As we headed down Century Avenue towards Jade's grandparent's home, I gently kissed her forehead and I could make out a smile of satisfaction playing on her lips.

This date might not have started off well, but in the end, it worked out okay and we both were happy. I was certain that we had a future to look forward to.

PART 3 – ALL GOOD THINGS

Chapter 19.   Fast Forward and Rewind

I was sitting in outside Starbucks by the bund. A gust of wind blew a strand of my now long hair over my eyes and gently grazed my nose. I brushed back the long and slightly greasy strand out of my face. My sunglasses ensured that the hair didn't get into my eyes. I took a sip of the hot black coffee and wiped the coffee out my scraggly moustache with the back of my hand.

Everyone else around me felt and made it obvious that I badly needed a haircut and shave, but for some reason, I didn't feel the same despite the fact that my hair had grown to shoulder length, and my beard was now very long and very unkept. I brushed my teeth every day, showered every day, shampooed my hair & beard, changed underwear every day, and wore clean clothes, which in my opinion was enough grooming.

The hangover was an intense one this time, and the coffee was barely helping. I was truly grateful that this was a weekend and not a weekday. It was time for a smoke. I lit up a cigarette, inhaled deep and started coughing violently almost immediately. I could taste the blood in my phlegm which I had coughed up. I looked around to ensure that no one was looking at me, spat out the phlegm into a rolled-up tissue and placed it into an empty cup left behind by another customer. My doctor had asked me to quit smoking since my mild asthma had aggravated to pneumonia, but I was obstinate about not quitting. I just continued to smoke and continued to take medication to "counter" the effects of smoking, which was, of course, stupid, but then so-called "love" makes some of us stupid and irrational.

Six months had passed since Jade left for Italy. Four months had passed since I discovered the truth. Since that day, I have been falling lower and lower with no bottom in sight.

It was really a beautiful day, and there were many couples and families out to enjoy the sun and the view. As was expected, there were a lot of tourists, enjoying the view on the bund and snapping pictures in various poses. There was a lot of happiness and laughter in the air, and there were a lot of happy kids running around.

All this happiness... It reminded me of my foolish happiness and the life I imagined with Jade. It just made me sick, and I had to get out of there. I stubbed out the cigarette and got up to leave.

As I stood up to leave, I felt woozy for a second and everything started blacking out. Just as I started losing my consciousness, I remembered that I had not eaten properly for four days now. I fell back heavily into the chair I was seated and pass out. The last thought in my head before losing my consciousness was, *I'm so fucked up.*

I woke up into an inky blackness. There was no up and down; there was no left and right; there was nothing, and I was suspended in the pitch-black blackness.

The blackness had engulfed me and it felt as if I was floating through space if that space was made of tar. This blackness penetrated every single pore and cell in my body. It was an icy cold, suffocating blackness which paralyzed my whole body and I couldn't move an inch. I struggled to breathe and break free, but the darkness had held me captive in its vice-like grip.

Some primal part of my brain screamed at me to wake up, but my eyes were sealed shut. The blackness had seeped into my lungs and I was struggling to breathe. My lungs were paralyzed and failed to respond to the most basic commands from the sub-conscious mind – Breath! I tried to scream for help and my jaw seemed to be held shut by the blackness.

My heart started beating harder and faster in panic and terror.

This terror was what brought me around, and I snapped awake. I gulped a few deep breaths to calm my heart down. I felt dizzy from passing out and, felt cold and clammy despite the weather outside being pleasant. Pneumonia and the asthma were acting up. I took out my inhaler and pumped a couple of doses of the medicine into my lungs and felt the airways opening up after a few laboured breaths.

It took me few moments to get my bearings and I realized that I was still at the Starbucks by the bund. The dream itself didn't really surprise me, as I had this recurring dream for the past three months since the first asthma attack. As the cloud in my brain further cleared up, I realized that the scene had not changed much since I passed out. By looking at the position of the sun, and at the time on my phone, I realized that I had passed out for less than five of minutes. It was still joyful, and there were still kids running around – generally, under normal circumstances, nothing changes in five minutes, but then your life can change in a blink of the eye. I started feeling sick at heart again as I was reminded of that painful memory.

I knew I had to get out of there, but I was starving and was worried that I would pass out again, this time on the way to the metro station. This would be a disaster as most of the people here wouldn't give a shit about a foreigner who has passed out on the footpath and in fact would avoid him or her like the plague. With that happy thought in my mind, I turned to pick up my bag and head indoors to buy some food. You may be surprised that my bag was not stolen, but then, given the state of my knapsack, I would be surprised if the bag was actually stolen.

The bag was over eight years old – very faded and very frayed. Despite the best efforts to clean the bag, it was covered with remnants of various stains accumulated over these years. In summary, it looked like something that came out of a garbage can or a landfill or something that the Salvation Army rejected. Combined with my dishevelled and nearly homeless look, even the most desperate of thief would have had serious second or third thoughts about stealing the bag. It just wasn't worth their effort.

I joined the queue at the Starbucks and ignored the stares of some of the people around me who were clearly wondering how a homeless Indian or Pakistani guy ended up in China or something along those lines. Clearly, I must have slipped through the visa and immigration gaps.

The people in front of me and behind me moved away from me and wrinkled their nose in disgust. I knew they were imagining smell emanating from my body, and I knew it was just their imagination. I had showered in the morning and had applied enough deodorant and perfumes in the morning to last me the whole day. I didn't care much as this perception effect helped me get seats in metro and helped cleared tables at coffee shops.

I ordered in Chinese, which apparently shocked the cashier and people behind me. I ordered a croissant, a coconut & hazelnut scone, and a cup of double shot latte. I paid with my Alipay app and requested the croissant and the scone to be warmed up.

As I waited for my order to be ready, I grabbed a few packets of sugar from the nearby counter, ripped open one of the packets and poured sugar into my mouth to ensure that I don't pass out again. This further attracted some glares of disdain from the patrons in the café. I wanted to show my middle finger to the people who thought they can judge me by my appearances and behaviours, but I made the effort to ignore these people.

After about five minutes the order was ready and I took the food out back to where I was sitting. The waiter had cleared out the cup I had left behind and replaced ashtray with a fresh one. I moved back to "my" now clean table. As I sat down in the seat I was seated before... the seat in which I had passed out in, I realized that my table was the last available table.

I started having the first decent meal in four days, not considering the booze and snacks I had ingested during this period of time. I added a packet of brown sugar to my coffee and stirred it until I was certain that the sugar had dissolved. I took a bite of the warm buttery croissant, and it was then I realized how hungry I really was. The croissant disappeared in less than a minute and I washed it down with the warm coffee. I sat there enjoying the sensation that was washing over my body... It was like having an orgasm, only better; the pleasure sensation was not localized and I felt my whole body come back to life. I wanted to smoke a cigarette but the pain in my chest told me I should hold off for some more time.

I was just about to attack the scone when I felt someone standing in front of me. I say "felt" as I didn't initially see who it was – I was so focussed on my scone that I didn't see anything else around me.

I raised my head to see a familiar face staring down at me. It was Nicole Zhang, standing there with a cup of coffee. But, there were no signs of recognition on her face, which was understandable as my appearances had changed drastically since we had last met. My jaw dropped open.

One might think that in a city teeming with 24 million people, such encounters should be rare, and nearly impossible. But, since most of us live a life of fixed routine and most of us have fixed preferences for the places we like to visit, it is not that unimaginable that our paths should intersect more often than one would imagine.

At least once a week, I would recognize a stranger during the metro ride to my office or would see a familiar face on my walk between metro and office. Now, some of you might say that all Chinese people look somewhat similar, but having lived in Shanghai long enough, I would first call you racist and then go on to tell you that I can differentiate most of the features. Once every while, I would see people I recognize in metro even on weekends, given that I liked to go to bund or *Huaihai* road or the *Jing'an* Area and it was entirely possible that these people also like to hang out in the same area. We live in a world of familiar strangers. The funny thing is, over the years I have stayed in China, I have come to believe that more strangers recognize me than I recognize them.

"Excuse me for interrupting", she said, "But, all the other seats are taken" She gestured around to bring to my attention, the fact that almost all the seats, except the ones at my table, were taken.

"If this place is not taken, and if you don't mind, may I sit here?" she added politely, still not recognizing me.

I clear my throat, and said, "Sure" as I nodded my head.

I was hoping that my voice might jog her memory, but no such luck. But then, all the smoking and the multiple bouts of pneumonia has changed my voice to be scratchier and deeper tone than before, so expecting her to recognize my voice was a bit of a stretch.

"Thank you", she replied with a polite smile and sat down gracefully. She placed the coffee on the table, sat down and fished out her MacBook Air, an 11-inch version. She opened the laptop, smiled at me again, turned to her laptop and went about her business.

I decided to stop staring as clearly, Nicole was nowhere close to recognizing me. The fact that I was wearing sunglasses probably didn't help in the recognition. I removed my glasses and placed on the table, hoping that would jog her memory. I blinked my eyes to adjust to the sudden flood of light. She was still deeply engrossed in whatever she was doing and didn't even look up.

As Nicole continued working, I quietly ate the scone and washed it down with some coffee. I studied the face of the person sitting across me, very carefully. I had to be sure that this is who I thought it was. It was the same perfect face, with the full lips, the perfect nose, the beautiful oval face, and the same sparkling black eyes... It was definitely, the one and only, Nicole Zhang... She had hardly changed. Which is normal, as people who live their normal lives wouldn't really change much in half a year, but for people who were going through hell, that half year might be equivalent of half a dozen years.

I honestly believed myself to be in the second category, someone going through living hell, but the fact that people have stopped recognizing me, made me question that belief... Then and there. Here is a person whom I had once believed would never forget me, would be a friend for the rest of my life and she has failed to recognise me. I had brooded all this while and refused to let go of my past; this has done nothing but ruins my health. I pushed away the people closest to me, people who really cared about me... People like my parents, my sister, my large family, my friends like Allen, or even someone like Nicole. Instead, I was trying to find an outlet for the madness I felt.

This was the moment of clarity.

I had to make the choice. I can finish the rest of the coffee and the scone, and I can leave quietly or I can talk to Nicole, remind her that it's me. I was given the opportunity to start the change then and there and it was a terrifying feeling. I had lived more or less like a hermit these past few months and I had lived the way I wanted to live. I had lived these past six months without having to answer to anyone. I had abused that situation and chose to lock myself in a dark place, unwilling to talk to friends and punishing myself... For a situation, I couldn't change. I had gotten really comfortable in my little world and the decision to come out that is really hard.

Why fix broken shit, only to be broken again?

The real question was, was I that broken? Or was it just a crack that hurt a lot? Or is it just that I need to be a little bit more courageous and deal with shit that happens in life. After all, I had come to the realization a while back, incidentally while talking to Nicole, that my pain is possibly nothing compared to the real mental and physical pain people go through their lives.

I ate the rest of my scone, drank rest of my coffee and pondered over these questions. I had a decent job. I can afford to eat three square meals. I have a decent home. I have money to spend on clothes and footwear. I have made the choice to punish myself and for what? For something I thought was my fault? At this point, I was not sure any more.

Nicole had looked up two times during the time I finished my scone, but she still failed to recognize me. I was done with the scone and nearly done with the coffee as well, and I had made up my mind. I should finish my coffee and leave. This was the best scenario that I could think of. I had no explanation for not talking to her all this while when she was seated right opposite to me. I can message her later.

I finished up the coffee, picked up my bag and got up to leave. As I stood up, Nicole looked up from the laptop and stared straight into my eyes. She smiled and gave me a polite nod. I returned the smile and the nod, and that instant I thought I saw a flicker of recognition or that of doubt passing over her face, but I decided not to stay there any further to find out what would happen next.

I started walking to the metro after leaving the Starbucks. I lit a cigarette and inhaled deeply. The pressure on the chest was back immediately and I started coughing violently. I dropped the cigarette and fished out my inhaler. As I pumped two doses the medicines into my lungs, I felt my phone vibrate. I ignored my phone and waited for my lungs relax. A minute later I had recovered.

Another moment of clarity – I need to quit smoking, so then and there, I decide to quit smoking. There were more than a dozen cigarettes left in the packet and an unopened packet in my bag, but I knew that if I tried to quit after I finished those cigarettes, like the way I had tried before, I most probably wouldn't be quitting any time soon. I had to grab this moment and hold on to it... This was quite possibly my last opportunity to quit smoking and start making changes to my life.

I had made up my mind.

I threw away the cigarettes and my favourite jet flame lighter into the nearest trash-can I could find. I immediately felt a huge weight lift off my mind. It was entirely possible that the feeling was more psychological than physiological, but for me, the feeling was as real as the cigarettes that I just threw away.

As the escalator took me up to the footbridge that connected Super Brand Mall to Lujiazui metro station, my phone vibrated again. I took out my phone out of the jeans pocket and unlocked it.

There were two messages.

One from Allen Huang and the other one, the more recent one from... Nicole Zhang. I blinked in disbelief after seeing that the message was from Nicole. For a moment, I thought I was hallucinating. The very next thought was if she was messaging inform me that she did recognize me and she was upset with the fact that I didn't possibly recognize her...

Rather than imagining up more scenarios, I tapped the message and opened it.

> Nicole Zhang (WeChat): Hey Anand, how you been? Hope you remember me. Well, I was thinking about you just now and realized that we have not talked in a while.

I was thinking of a response to Nicole message when I got a second message from her.

> Nicole Zhang (WeChat): If you are free tomorrow, do you want to meet for a brunch? We can meet at the Blue Frog or TGI Fridays near the bund.

The mention of the TGI Friday stopped my heart for a moment. The memory of my date with Jade came rushing back and I started feeling dizzy again. I stopped walking, stood there taking deep breaths and waited for the dizziness to pass. After the dizziness had passed, surprisingly, I was not feeling angry or sad. While I cannot accurately describe the feeling, I would say that it felt like acceptance.

> Anand Nair (WeChat): Hey Nicole, long time no see. I definitely do remember

```
you :-). I am doing okay. Strangely,
I was just thinking about you too.
Let's meet at Blue Frog near the bund
tomorrow. What time would you want to
meet?
```

I waited for the reply from Nicole and entered the Lujiazui metro station. As I got on to the escalator that led passengers down to the underground metro platform, Nicole's response came in.

```
Nicole Zhang (WeChat): :-) Are you
okay to meet by 11:00?
```

I replied immediately before she changed her mind.

```
Anand Nair (WeChat): Sure. 11 Sounds
perfect. See you tomorrow :-).
```

I got an immediate response from Nicole.

```
Nicole Zhang (WeChat): See you
tomorrow :-).
```

When I swiped the metro card and entered the metro station, I realized that I was actually smiling, and if I were, to be honest with myself, it felt good to start moving forward rather than being obsessed with the past. It's not that I have not smiled and laughed all this while, but this one came from a place deep within. I was afraid of feeling too happy, just to have it smashed to bits later, but still, I enjoyed the feeling at that moment.

My train arrived a few moments later, I got into the train and checked the message from Allen, though I knew it was another invite from him to go over to his place for dinner and drinks. I accepted his invitation, but this time I genuinely wanted to meet him and Jean, and not just to keep up with the appearances.

I guess it is time now to take a step back and connects the dots since Jade left to Italy to the day at Starbucks, six months after. Time to rewind the tape... Time to go back six months.

Chapter 20.   The Day After the Dinner Date

I woke up feeling refreshed the next day, the day after the dinner date, at around 7:00 AM, even though I had slept only at around 2:00 AM. I guess it had to do with the fact that it was Monday and it was a holiday. Not working on a Monday is itself a refreshing thought but having had the night I had the Monday felt even sweeter.

The previous night, I had reached home around half past 8, had taken another cold shower and changed into my night gear. I had put on a hoodie, stepped out on to the balcony and started smoking a cigarette to help me think about what I should do.

I really didn't want to wait for three weeks, until Jade came back, but I didn't want to look desperate by committing right away. I tried imagining what would happen if Jade were to change her mind, and it was a painful thought.

I would be left in a place where I wouldn't be able to meet Jade, see her laughter, hold her, make love to her, share a quiet moment with her, have dinner dates with her, travel around the world with her and perhaps even spend the rest of my life with Jade. I loved the fact that I was living the moment, most of the time, whenever I am with Jade. This is something I felt I can do with for the rest of my life.

The question really was, was Jade the right person for me and vice versa. I know her, but then how well do I really know her and vice versa, how well do Jade really know me. She had admitted that she used to be superficial and cared only about money, and If I were, to be honest with myself I was also superficial in the sense, I was attracted to the beauty of Jade Lin. It was also possible that I was looking for security in the known.

Another thing that really was a factor was the fact that I was insecure about my looks and I feared that I will never find anyone as attractive as Jade. I felt ashamed of this small, selfish, and superficial thought.

I tried to push all these thoughts out of my mind, but they just kept coming back to me like a bad penny, until these thoughts started going in a circle. This cyclone of thoughts was dissipated by the phone vibrating in my pocket. I unlocked my phone to find that I had a WeChat message from Jade.

```
Jade Lin (WeChat): I hope you reached
home, Anand. Thank you for the
wonderful evening, I really enjoyed
spending time with you. I will miss
you when I am away. I will miss
holding you and kissing you. Please
wait for me... I will be back before
you know it.
```

This message washed away some of my insecurities and my shame, as the message was a sign that I shouldn't doubt myself too much and try to live the moment. I took a deep breath and immediately typed out a response to Jade.

```
Anand Nair (WeChat): I am home Jade.
I had a great evening too. I will
miss you too. I really meant it when
I said that I wanted to give our
relationship a shot. I don't think I
can spend a day without you. Please
go to sleep now XOXO.
```

I was hoping that Jade would respond immediately, but instead, I waited about 45 seconds staring the screen looking at the word 'Typing', on top of the chat screen. I

I think my eyes had glazed over as I waited for the response because I felt the message before I saw it.

```
Jade Line (WeChat): Anand, I think...
I love you.
```

I was blown away by this message and nearly dropped my phone. My heart started racing at the implication of what she said. She said "I love you" and for people in our age group, that phrase means a lot. It meant she had very strong feelings for me, or she had some mental problems, but I didn't want to latter case.

In any case, I decided to wait for two minutes, just to ensure that Jade wouldn't recall the message after realizing that she might have committed too early.

The two-minute wait turned to a five-minute wait, just to ensure that she had an opportunity to change her mind. I guess, she was starting to worry now because, after six minutes, she sent me three messages, one after the other, and I could almost sense the panic she was feeling.

```
Jade Line (WeChat): Anand, are you
okay?

Jade Line (WeChat): Did I say
something wrong?

Jade Line (WeChat): Did I just screw
up even before we got started? I am
so sorry... I just thought you felt
the same way as I felt and I was done
waiting for you to say it :-(.
```

This flood of message snapped me into action and I messaged her back.

```
Anand Nair (WeChat): No No, nothing
like that. I feel the same way and I
didn't know how to express this to
you without seeming like I'm rushing
things. I think I love you too Jade.
I want nothing more than being with
you, and possibly spending the rest
of my life with you.
```

Now, instead of texting back, Jade video called me on WeChat. Now, I did mention earlier that I had some reservations about video chatting on WeChat as a replacement for real human connection, but when I saw Jade in her nightdress staring at me on that phone screen, I sort of changed my mind and thought, *I can make this work for three weeks*. She looked stunning and she was glowing with happiness.

"Anand", Jade said, her voice and her face full of emotions, "Did you just tell me that you want to spend the rest of your life with me?"

I really hadn't thought about it that way when I said that I wanted to spend "the rest of my life with" her, but I knew in my heart this is what I wanted.

"I guess, I just did", I replied, blushing and smiling from ear to ear.

"Oh, this is moving too fast," She mumbled with a distant look on her face. She seemed to be thinking about what we should do next. She seemed happy and conflicted at the same time. She had that look that which meant she was about to speak her mind. The smile on my face had faded off and was replaced with a frown.

"Anand, I would like that as well, but let's take this one step at a time. I want us to know the good and bad sides of each other. I don't want you to be telling me this because I voiced what I feel for you", she said after about a minute.

"Right now, I know how we feel for each other and this is a great start, but I don't want to get into a long-term commitment without experiencing more of the real life with you. Right this moment, I love you, I know that. I have learnt the hard way, that being in love for a moment is easy, but staying in love for weeks, months, years… for the rest of life, which is nearly impossible and takes a lot of effort and mutual understanding. I want us to build this up… travel together, live together, make life decisions together and see how best we can tolerate each other", she added before I could refute her earlier argument.

I paused a minute and tried to imagine things from her perspective. She had gone through a nasty divorce and that is the sort of thing that will leave a permanent scar, no matter how courageous or strong one might be. She would obviously want to take things slow and understand me as a person a little bit more. Sure, our chemistry was out of the world and I knew that we liked being with each other physically, but that really shouldn't define the relationships. After all, we live in a society where sex is a mechanical activity like getting drunk once in a while or going for a weekend trip, but to start a relationship under the premise and guidance of quality sex was… for the lack of better words, idiotic.

"You are right, Jade", I said, summarizing my thoughts, and emphasized, "We should take some time to think about all the aspects of our lives".

She had a smile on her face and I wished that we were together, even it is for just five minutes, so that I could hold her and kiss her.

"I really wish that I could be there with you now", Jade said, voicing my thought for both of us.

"When will you stop reading my thoughts?" I asked, half joking, half serious, and fully knowing what the response would be.

"You know the answer for that", she replied, with a knowing smile on her face.

"I liked to hear that from you", I responded, fully knowing that she was playing with me.

"Alright", she said with an exaggerated sigh, but smiling, "As long as we are together, I am never going to stop doing that – reading your thoughts."

"And, you better not", I said, smiling broadly.

I heard a lady's voice in the background asking Jade to go to sleep early. Jade turned and responded in Chinese, that she will be turning in soon,

Before she could convey that message to me, I jumped in and said, "Listen, you need to get up early tomorrow. Please go to sleep now. I will text you in the morning."

She smiled and said, "Yes, I need to sleep now. You please go back to sleep and we can talk like this once I am in Palermo. I love you and I miss you".

"Good night darling, Have a safe journey tomorrow. I love you too", I said, giving a wave of my hand.

"Good night, my dear Anand. Take care", she said before ending the call.

I wanted to sleep immediately, and I went to bed after I smoked another cigarette, but for some reason, sleep didn't come that easily. I kept tossing and turning for the next few hours until sleep came to me around 2 AM in the morning. I had this feeling of unease, a sense of foreboding, but I couldn't put a finger on the feeling. But, when the sleep finally came to me, I slept a deep, dreamless sleep.

So, that was last night.

Now, Jade should be on the way to the airport with her family or already at the airport.

I was still in my bed when I checked my phone to see if there were any messages from Jade and there were indeed two messages from Jade and one message from Nicole.

I opened up the message from Jade, which she has sent in the morning. Nicole's message could wait for some time.

> Jade Lin (WeChat): Hey Anand, we are on our way to the airport, will be reaching soon. I didn't sleep much last night. I was thinking of us the whole night. I almost wanted to come to your home and spend some time with you. What I am trying to say is, I miss you very much and I love you. I want you to take your time and think about what we talked about the last night.
>
> Jade Lin (WeChat): I will get a local number once I'm in Italy. I will message or call on WeChat from a Wi-Fi hotspot until then. Take care of yourself, dear.

This was sent just two minutes before I woke up. I almost started feeling guilty that I slept better than Jade. I wanted to lie about sleeping, but after thinking for about five minutes, I knew that I shouldn't. I didn't want to start the relationship based on lies. Experience has shown that it takes the relationship nowhere.

We start a relationship based on lies and try to show our best sides to the other person because we fear that our relationship wouldn't succeed otherwise. This is probably one of the biggest reasons relationship fails; people really don't know the truth until they were deep into the relationships and when the truth comes out, there is a sense of betrayal.

The size of betrayal varies. It might be a something relatively small, like an email address that the partner didn't know about or a second phone number that the spouse didn't know about. It might be a larger betrayal, like an active Ashley Madison or Tinder profile or other sexual partners or a serious drug habit or an anger problem that the partner was unaware of. Whatever is the case, all these little and big betrayals add up, and destroys the relationship, leading to breaks up and nasty divorces.

So, I replied with the truth.

```
Anand Nair (WeChat): Good morning
darling, I couldn't sleep until about
2 AM. I was thinking about us as well.
It's very difficult for me to be away
from you, but I guess we both need
this to really figure out where we
are going. Try and get some sleep on
the flight, and message me when
possible. I don't want you to text
when you are with your folks. Safe
flight to you and your folks. I too
miss you and love you.
```

I didn't wait for the reply and got out the bed to get ready for the day. I made a coffee and smoked a cigarette in the balcony before I hit the toilet. I had forgotten about Nicole message. I had a cold shower and got ready for the day. I wanted to go to the Puxi side of the bund and take a long walk, as this helped me think. It was still cold, so I had dressed in layers.

I made a protein shake with oats, protein powder, avocado, chia seeds and partially skimmed milk and took it to my dining table. I checked my phone to see if Jade has responded and she had indeed replied, during the time I was dressing up.

```
Jade Lin (WeChat): We at the airport
now waiting to check in. I will text
you once we are done.

Anand Nair (WeChat): Okay baby.
Message when you can. I am off to
Puxi side of the bund to take a walk.
Take care.

Jade Lin (WeChat): :-) You have fun.
Take care.
```

Chapter 21.   The Long Walk

I took a Mobike to the metro station and the metro to the Lujiazui station. From there I walked to the pier on Fucheng road to and took the ferry across the Huangpu River to the Puxi side. If the ferry was crowded, as it tends to be during the holidays, I really didn't notice, as the playlist I was listening to at the time had blocked out most of the noise, and my mind busy with the thoughts of how to take forward the relationship with Jade, helped block out the rest of the reality.

By the time I reached Puxi side of the bund, I was on auto-pilot. Only my thoughts for Jade and I existed.

While walking along the promenade, I got a message from Jade letting me know they finished the security check and will be boarding the flight soon. I wished them a safe travel. She texted again just before turning off her phone. I replied to her that I am eagerly waiting for her to return. I think she had turned off the phone by then, as I didn't get any reply to those messages, not that my messages warranted any replies.

My walk took me to Shanghai People's Heroes Memorial Tower, where I turned around and tracked back to the ferry stop and started walking towards the Nanpu Bridge Metro station. Once I reached Nanpu Bridge Station, instead of taking the metro, I walked back to the ferry stop, from where I walked down the East Nanjing Pedestrian street, crossed over the people square and walked to JingAn temple.

All this while, I tried to think about my long-term prospects with Jade Lin. I let my logical brain take over and analyse the pros and cons of the situation I was in.

Despite the fact that Jade was a familiar person to me, I really didn't know her that well. While she's beautiful, smart and intelligent, and our chemistry was fantastic, I was yet to see a real reason to be with Jade for the rest of my life. When I made a decision to sleep with her, my main motivation was sex, nothing less, nothing more. In all honesty, I had been sex deprived for a long time. Since Jade was sexually attracted to me some time back and since she was alone in a noodle shop in the middle of the night, I had rolled the dice when we waited for the taxi at Xintiandi the previous night to see what would happen. It worked out in my favour.

I liked her, and I loved her external appearances, but is that enough to get into commitment or love her for the rest of my life as I had previously thought? I had some glimpses of the way she thought and acted, and from what I could see of that very thin slice, she was a good person. I cannot really be worried about her past as, at our age, everyone has had some kind of experiences, good or bad and it's really difficult to find someone without any baggage. I consider myself, in most cases, a good and an honest person, but even I had not talked about my past and my baggage, except for my brother's story.

What if, deep in my subconscious, I had seen Jade as a way out of a middle-class life? While I was not poor by any stretch of the imagination, I wasn't rich either and I wouldn't even call myself upper-middle-class, the way my father described our family. I was afraid that I started "loving" Jade for her money after I came to know about her inheritance. I was not such a person before, as I never cared too much for money, but then people can change over time.

You spend all your life working hard hoping that one day you will "make it". Often you discover very late that, most people like yourself, lived pay-check to pay-check, not because they are not intelligent or because they are not smart, but because they lack the courage to take the leap – They fear failure, they fear adversity and they let the fear paralyse them and force them to hold on to comforts of safety.

I feared failure and adversity as much as the next man. I would love to say that I have done things that pushed my horizons, and rolled a lot of dices, but the fact is that I haven't taken any real risks in my life. The fact that I stayed so long in Shanghai is the absolute proof that I was terrified of change and I didn't like uncertainty. For people looking from outside, the feeling is that I have braved the odds, learnt the language, got an MBA degree and found success in a place like Shanghai, whereas the reality was I was desperately holding on to the familiar comforts of a known devil. The point is, while I was not a gold digger, I really have to find a way to take money out of the equation while thinking about Jade.

I chain-smoked three cigarettes while thinking about this and came to the conclusion that I really didn't care about how much money Jade had inherited. I knew this, as I had dated women with more money and lesser money and I had never let that come in way of feeling that I developed for them. It was really a non-factor in the relationship for me. I was happy that Jade had a bunch of money, but I was going to work hard to make sure that she has everything that her heart desires, should we get into a long-term relationship.

At the same time, I came to the conclusion that her Italian passport is not a factor as well for me in this relationship, although if she wanted, I was okay to make the move to Europe, even if the opportunities might be a bit lesser for me.

I also concluded that I might have declared my love for her a little too quickly and the fact of the matter was – I liked her a lot, I was sexually attracted to her, and that I need some more time before deciding if I did love her, and more importantly If I wanted us to spend a lifetime together. I made a mental note to ensure that, I talk about this to Jade, whenever we video chatted the next time.

All this while I was thinking about this from my point of view, and it felt a little selfish to me. I tried putting myself in Jade's shoes, realized that it's possible that she was trying to scratch the seven-year itch she felt for me way back then. Now that, that itch is scratched, does she have a real reason to be with me?

When she said, she loved me, what exactly did she mean? What if she hadn't really thought this through? But the fact that she wanted to take slow and get to know me better, was a good sign for me, as it meant she has actually thought about this for some time, as she said before. This also meant that when she professed her love for me, it possibly came from a place deep within. It is also possible that she was scared that I might walk off if she didn't say those words, as sex might hold a different, a less scared, and meaning to me. She might have intuited that I have been sex deprived and was rolling the dice when I made the move and kissed her. She might have also guessed from the way we made love, that I was attracted to her and liked her.

This was truly a confusing thought with many circular, chicken and egg sort of questions.

I tried thinking from the perspective of our respective parents. My parents were at that point where they would be happy if I found a girl to share my life with, preferably through the bonds of marriage. They really didn't care where the girl was from but requested me to marry someone who wouldn't force me to change my religion. I was fairly certain that Jade doesn't practice any religion, but even if she did, she didn't seem like a person who would force her religion on anyone else. I knew this, as she never talked about religion.

I knew that I faced an uphill challenge when it comes to convincing Jade's mother, as her mom and her daughter have themselves gone through a divorce. It would only be fair for Jade's mother to be worried about her daughter being with a foreigner, that too an Indian. Since marrying a rich Chinese didn't really work out for Jade, her mother might be willing to give an Indian a chance. In any case, I knew that eventually when I had to talk to Jade's mother and her Chinese grandparents, it will be a challenge due to one reason or the other. I really had no idea how they felt about Indians in general and what their thoughts are about this particular Indian. I hoped that, if and when the time came, my Chinese language skills would help... somewhat.

There is the question of what my friends would think, should they find out how quickly we professed the love for each other. I was immediately ashamed of this thought as, if I loved Jade, I shouldn't fear what the 'society' thinks about us.

I also started thinking about my health and Jade's health and realized that we shouldn't be smoking so much should we were to have a long and healthy life together. I decided that I should try to give up smoking during these three weeks and set an example for Jade. I still had about a pack and a half of cigarettes remaining and I promised myself that I will quit smoking as soon as I finished the remaining cigarettes.

In the end, I decided that she may love me, or the version of me she knew from seven years back and the one she slept with, but she hasn't seen all sides of me. She will need some time to see that. She will have to know what my real background was, what my real values are and I will have to do the same for Jade.

This holiday break would be a good time for both of us also to think about what we wanted from each other and think about what really needs to be done one once we are back together.

I had reached the JingAn metro station, a few minutes after the long train of my thoughts, had come to a halt. As I entered the metro station, I came to the conclusion that I had to convey some of these thoughts to Jade and I didn't really want to wait until I talked to Jade directly, as God alone knew when that would happen.

I opened my quip app and started writing out the message to Jade. I thought I would be done by the time I got into the next train, but I had totally underestimated my capacity to ramble when I'm writing down my thoughts. I was already crossing over to the Pudong side of the river, and nowhere near completing the message.

On a whim, I got out at the Dongchang road station. I headed to Blue Frog located at the basement of the Shanghai World Financial Centre to have a drink or two – because the happy hour was starting in less than five minutes – and complete my message to Jade.

Chapter 22. A Long Text Message

Two gin martinis later, the message was done, and it was way longer than expected. I had expected to get this done in less than half an hour but had finally spent close to two hours writing that message.

I had two choices, send one very long message on WeChat or send her an email. I decided that I will do both, in case either of us accidentally deletes the WeChat message.

Instead of sending the message directly, over the next hour, I broke it into paragraphs and ensured that I didn't make any obvious spelling or grammatical error. I then pasted each paragraph into to the chat box and send them one by one.

I got Jade's email address from her Facebook profile and send the whole message, which was more like a thought dump, as an email.

From: Anand Nair

To: Jade Lin

Subject: A Few Thought and Ramblings (A Reproduction of the WeChat Messages I Sent You)

Dear Jade,

I just wanted to send the message I sent you as an email to ensure that you get the message and you can read it easily as an email. I got your email address from your Facebook profile.

I hope you are getting enough rest on the flight. I just finished a long walk and now I am in the Blue Frog located in the basement of SWFC.

As I walked along bund and streets of Shanghai, I was thinking about how fate or the universe or some higher power brought us back together, especially at a time where we needed each other. It was clearly meant to happen, why else would we run into each other in that noodle restaurant, a place where we had the least likelihood of meeting on a Saturday night.

Whenever I think of you, I am reminded of the wonderful time we spent together. You are always in my thoughts ever since we first met, all those years back, and now, you have a permanent place in my heart. I hope you feel the same way about me.

During the walk, I had an opportunity to ponder your point about thinking hard about spending our lives together, and I think you are right. Such decisions cannot be made so suddenly, as we live in a world where relationships are becoming more and more complex and nothing is truly certain.

It is important that we both think hard about this.

Previous experiences would have shown us that we try to show our best to the other at the beginning of the relationship because we are afraid of losing each other. Fear as a foundation for any relationship would only lead to disaster in the future. I believe, after much thought, we should take time to discover each other's weaknesses as well as the bad sides.

You told me about your divorce and it was then I realized that we both had our share of bad relationships even before we had met each other. I should have told you about my own failed marriage, and I had many opportunities to talk about, but somehow this slipped my mind or I just couldn't find the courage to talk about this. Better late than never… I guess.

This happened when I was 27, and I had just got married to the love of my life, whom I had known for seven years. I thought I knew her well, only to discover within the week of our marriage, she would rather be with her lover. I found out about this in the most painful way, after she eloped with her lover, on the seventh day after getting married. She sent me a text informing me that she cannot live without her lover whom she had met six months back at work.

I was mentally destroyed and filed for an annulment of marriage. I took the first available opportunity to leave India and by the end of the year, I was in Shanghai.

The lesson learnt for me was that 'love' can be a fickle thing, and only plays a small part in the success of any relationship. We need to be able to develop trust and respect between the partners in the relationship. We need to be able to accept people for who they are without focussing on their shortcomings, as nobody is perfect. We need to find a way to keep falling in love again and again with the same person so that we will not need anyone else and we can have a happy life together, for the rest of our lives.

Having said that I really don't want us to be starting this relationship with a lie. I really want you to know that I like you a lot and I adore you, but I may have panicked when you told me you love me and replied the same way. I want to love you and I am hoping that I will fall in love with you a thousand times over so that we can be together... forever. Don't think that I don't care for you or I want to hurt you. It's only because I care for you I want to be honest.

I want us to be together... if possible, for the rest of our lives, but let us both take a step back and be very sure of this. I want us to experience life together and maybe even live together for a while.

I miss you terribly and I am eagerly waiting for you to come back into my arms.

Anand

After I sent the email, I texted Jade and told her that I have sent the same message as an email to the address she used for registering her Facebook.

I really needed some food in my stomach now, as the booze was going to my head.

I ordered a medium done cheeseburger minus the onions and tomatoes and swapped the fries out for a salad. I wanted to start focussing on my health and I wanted to make changes to my lifestyle right away.

As I ate my burger I realized that I still had to check the messages from Allen. I opened the chat and responded to it immediately. He had invited me for a get-together the weekend after the next. I immediately accepted the invitation and promised I would be there. He told me that he wanted all the details from the past couple of day. In his own words, "not the summary, but the complete details".

I headed back home after the burger, took a shower and turned in for the night. I put my phone into Airplane mode and made a mental note to check Nicole's message in the morning. It might be just a message, but once every while, that message will trigger a long conversation, that would ruin my sleep or even the whole night. I guess we all had similar experiences in our life before.

Shanghai – A Year to Remember

Chapter 23.   While Waiting for A Response

The next day, I woke up at around 8:00 AM, and decided that I should start the day with my usual workout. I managed to complete the workout in just under 40 minutes.

After my usual ablutions, I made my breakfast and while eating my breakfast, opened up the phone to check if there were any messages and discovered that I had two well-spaced messages from Jade sent sometime during the night.

The first message was a normal message, which probably meant that she hadn't read my long message yet.

> Jade Lin (WeChat): Hey Anand, we reached Palermo safely. The flight was good and I managed to get some sleep. I saw that you were messaging like crazy, let me read then and text you back. I love you and I miss you like crazy, my darling.

About an hour later she texted back, presumably after reading my long text or email.

> Jade Lin (WeChat): Anand, thank you for being honest. You are right we need to take it slow and we need to get to know each other well, given our pasts. I know what I feel for you is true, you take your time to decide dear. Take care.

That was that. There were no messages after. I didn't know what the last message meant. Did I make a mistake by telling the truth? Did I panic and say that I might not love Jade whereas what I felt for her was, truly love? I shook all these thoughts and feelings as I knew that I had to remain strong.

I went through the messages Jade sent me again and to me, it felt like she's willing to give me some time and space to decide how do we go forward, so I decided to keep my reply simple.

> Anand Nair (WeChat): Take care, Jade. I am sure that everything will work out. I miss you.

I waited for about five minutes for a response, but it was stupid as Jade was probably sleeping.

I had nearly finished the breakfast when I remembered that I still had an unread message from Nicole. I tapped open her WeChat message and read it. She had sent this message an hour before Jade had messaged me on her way to the airport, the day before.

> Nicole Zhang (WeChat): Hi, Anand. How are you? I am sorry about cancelling on you the last minute. If you are free tomorrow, can we meet up at the Element Fresh for lunch or dinner? I hope to meet you in person and talk more.

Since she had sent this on the day before and since it was too late for a lunch now, I knew I should check with her for dinner. I texted her back immediately.

> Anand Nair (WeChat): Hey Nicole. Apologies for not responding earlier, I was caught up in something. If you are free today evening, can we meet

> for dinner? I am okay with whichever place you choose.

She texted back in the next five minutes or so.

> Nicole Zhang (WeChat): Hi, Anand. No worries. If you are okay, can we meet at Blue Frog in 96 Plaza by 6:00 PM. This is the one near Century Avenue Station. Let us catch the happy hour there.

I texted back to confirm my availability and I got the reply almost immediately.

> Anand Nair (WeChat): Sounds good to me and I know the place. See you there at six :-).
>
> Nicole Zhang (WeChat): See you soon, Anand :-).

If it were any other day, I would have been really happy with the outcome of this conversation, but my mind was really on Jade and was trying to think what was going through her mind. There was nothing I could do until Jade replied back.

I decided to clean my apartment and organise things around my house to keep my mind off Jade Lin and stop thinking about how our relationship was going to pan out.

Cleaning the house was a soothing, meditative experience for me, and it generally helped me to keep my mind off whatever was troubling me. I vacuumed the house twice and mopped the floor twice, not because the house was dirty, but because of the therapeutic effect, it had on me. This was no different and I nearly forgot about my love troubles. I finished my clean-up by organising my pile of DVD, which took way longer than I expected.

I was really sweaty and smelly from the workout as well as from cleaning and organizing my house. I needed a shower. I guess Jade will see the message when she will see the message and she will do what she will have to do when she feels like it.

I took a long, freezing cold shower to wash out all the weariness out of my body. The icy needles of water washed away sweat from my body. It helped me relax further even though I was shaking and shivering from the freezing cold.

After nearly five minutes in the cold shower, my body couldn't take it anymore. I walked out the shower, shaking to the core and towelled myself dry vigorously. Despite the fact that the bathroom was cold, I felt a rush of warmth due to the temperature differential. I got into the bedroom and dressed up quickly. I was still shivering a bit even after dressing up, so I turned up the heat a couple of degrees.

I sat on the edge of the bed and checked my phone for messages. Jade hadn't responded to my text. There were some group messages that I cleared out as most of the message were in Chinese and reading all those messages will take me forever. There was a message from Nicole.

```
Nicole Zhang (WeChat): Hi, Anand. I
was thinking of biking to 96 Plaza.
Do you want to bike with me? I will
leave by 5:30 PM.
```

I didn't know what to think of that offer. It's after all only a bike ride and I had nothing to lose from this. It was better than her cancelling on me, again.

```
Anand Nair (WeChat): Hey Nicole. I am
good with that. I can take a Mobike.
I will meet you at your community
gate by 5:30 PM.
```

The reply was near instantaneous like she was waiting for a reply.

```
Nicole Zhang (WeChat): See you near
the East Gate by Huamu Road :-).
```

I got ready by 5:15 PM and got out of my community to find a Mobike. I managed to find one with an adjustable seat, and I unlocked the bike by scanning the QR code. I checked my phone for a message from Jade and she still hadn't messaged. I rode the bike up the road to the entrance of Nicole's community and waited by the gate for Nicole to show up.

She came out at exactly at 5:30 PM and she was riding her own city bike. She was wearing a burgundy turtleneck sweater and a pair of black jeans. She also was wearing a white down jacket with a hoodie to protect her from the cold. She saw me and waved at me and rode her bike towards me. She looked happy even from this distance.

"Hey Anand, Good to see you", she said with this huge smile on her face, "Sorry, I had to change the plans so many times."

"Hey Nicole, it is good to see you too", I replied and added "Don't worry about it. I am happy that we could meet."

I was actually feeling happy with the change in scenery and decided that I am not going to let thoughts of Jade get in way of this dinner. Whatever happens, is beyond my control now and my thought was that I should accept the outcome no matter what. I could, of course, have recalled the message, or not sent the email, but now it's a little too late.

Just when I was about to space out thinking about how not to space out, Nicole's phone dinged loudly then. She muted the phone and apologised for the intrusion.

I dismissed the apology but did the same with my phone as I had a feeling that Jade was not going to message me and even if she messaged me, it might be something that I didn't want to hear.

Avoidance can sometimes help you deal with bad situations.

We started biking towards Blue Frog and I just followed Nicole as I had never biked to 96 Plaza. She seemed familiar with the route and we reached there around 5:45 PM, after illegally riding the bike on roads where you are not allowed to ride bikes. Nicole had to hunt around to find a parking spot for her bike, as she needed to lock the bike. She locked her bike using one chain lock and a normal bike lock, both of which you can find in any Decathlon store in Shanghai.

I just locked the bike to end my ride and ensured that I got the signature triple beeps (beep-beep-beep) confirming that the bike was locked. I checked my phone to confirm that the payment has been made. I sneaked a peek at my WeChat to see if there were any messages and there were none.

Some promises, especially to yourself, are hard to keep. Like promises to lose weight, go to the gym, eat healthy, drink less, or quit smoking – for some people like me, it never happens.

I put my phone back into my pocket and I walked with Nicole to the Blue Frog. We found a table as soon as we reached there and we were seated quickly.

I ordered a Blue Frog Long Island Ice Tea and a Mexican Burger, minus onions and tomatoes, with a side of sweet potato fries with mayonnaise and mustard. Sweet potato fries are 'healthier' in my opinion, so that was a win.

Nicole ordered a Blue Frog mojito and a Caesar salad. If she wasn't so beautiful, I would have hated her for making me feel guilty for ordering such an unhealthy dinner.

As we waited for the drink to come, Nicole apologised again for cancelling out on me.

"I had some emergency work that came to me. It was a big opportunity so, I didn't want to turn it down", she said apologetically.

"Don't worry about it, we have all been in such situations", I said not really caring about the cancellation as it gave me an opportunity to spend some time with Jade before she left.

"So, is this opportunity something you want to talk about?", I followed up as the curiosity got the best of me.

Her face lit up with happiness and Nicole looked like she was going to burst with joy. Our drinks just arrived around then and she took a sip of her drink and launched right into to her story.

She explained how on Saturday evening how one of her friends in the venture capitalist or the VC space had messaged her asking her if she was looking for investors to scale up her business. This was one of the bigger names in the industry and she wanted to meet the guy to understand what was on the table.

They had planned their meeting on Monday afternoon and she was not sure when she would be able to complete the discussion, which is why she postponed the meeting a couple of times.

She had spent the whole of Sunday and the Monday morning preparing her business plan, including her marketing plan, competitor analysis, financial and future expansion plans. The meeting with her VC friend went well and the company is interested in investing in her company, especially since she was developing a digital strategy for her company. I was truly happy for her, as she seemed to be very committed to what she was doing.

I was a bit distracted as I couldn't stop thinking about Jade. I was itching to check my phone to see if Jade had messaged back. Although I was smiling on the outside, I not very happy. I was conflicted. It appeared that Jade and I didn't understand each other well, and we were off on the wrong foot. She proclaimed her love for me without expecting anything, only to have me do the same and back off in less than twenty-four hours.

When Jade and I were with each other, we were in the moment, but my problem was that, when I am not with her, my mind was all over the place, and I was filled with insecurities. Out of site, was not really out of mind. When I am not with her, I obsessively thought about her... Jade was like an addiction for me.

Perhaps, we need some time to understand each other better. We are different people after all. There was another thought in my mind, which I chose to ignore – that perhaps Jade and I aren't a good fit for various reasons, including but not limited to the way we think about each other's way of thinking. Perhaps, we should accept that we are oil and water and would never be suitable for each other no matter what we do.

But... Jade is not here now, so I forced myself to focus on now and the present.

Nicole was talking about the digital strategy for her company and I was pleasantly surprised to find out that she had done quite an amount of research and groundwork. This being something I was familiar with, I started walking her through the product plan and convinced her that she should really focus on the Minimum Viable Product or the MVP rather than going all in.

As we ate our dinners, Nicole and I discussed what should go into the

MVP for her product. For her students, the foundation material she developed, along with her unique teaching methods, especially for English and Analytical reasoning were the unique proposition for her students. Apparently, the materials were so good that some of the unscrupulous competitors were copying her material. So, we decided that MVP should include a secure digital delivery system for these materials so as to help build a strong user base, ensure "customer stickiness" and the security of the system.

She was convinced that she should add an analytics platform in the backend (or what the customer doesn't see) to improve the effectiveness of the system. Again, I was blown away by the fact that she has thought about a lot of things a usual small business owner wouldn't think about. She was already thinking like an entrepreneur. We discussed more on this aspect and decided to adopt the MVP approach for this as well, electing to depend on freely available open source tools to manage the analytics part until the business is big enough.

We discussed a lot of ideas and I found that I was able to contribute to the discussion without having to think too hard. The thoughts and conversation just flowed. This felt good, having a conversation without being scared of what may or may not be the reaction. Just a couple of friends having a conversation, that's all.

By the time we finished our dinner and the second round of drinks from the happy hour, it was well past 9:00 PM and we were thinking about ordering the third round. I realized that I didn't want to check my message and see if Jade had replied.

I was having too good a time to worry about that and if that was selfish, so be it. I was game for the third round of drink so was Nicole, so we repeated the order.

I could see that Nicole was happy because of the discussion we just had, and she seemed willing to talk more. It might also be the alcohol loosening her tongue and lowering her usual barriers. Probably a good time to find out why she freaked out on the metro. I gently broached the subject once our drinks were served.

"So, Nicole, do you want to talk about what happened on the train the other day?" I asked as she took a sip of the drink.

If she was surprised or shocked by the abrupt change in subject, it didn't really show on her face. The smile was gone for sure, so I knew it was something bad, though I was not sure how bad. I really had a bad timing and never really thought about what to say before I opened my damn mouth.

Nicole started stirring her drink, and she appeared to be trying to put words to her thought. She took a long sip of her drink before she talked again.

"My parents died in the Wenzhou train collision in 2011", she said matter-of-factly after about a minute of stirring the drink. I needed no further explanation, as to why she was so shook-up the other day. I was actually surprised that she was holding on to her composure so well now and that she still uses trains for her commute.

The Wenzhou train collision happened on July 2011, on a viaduct in the suburbs of Wenzhou, derailing two high-speed trains and had led to about 40 deaths. I never thought I would ever meet someone who had such a close connection to the incident.

"I am truly sorry for your loss, and I am truly an idiot to bring this up", I apologised as sincerely as possible.

She shook her head to convey it is not my fault, "It's okay. I never told you anything about my parents."

While that might be true, I felt really guilty about it. I barely knew her and it felt like I had crossed a line. I would probably never know how that loss felt like. I had lost a brother to an accident but to lose both your parent at the same time was nothing but unthinkable. Also, she was dealing with it far better than I could ever deal with such a loss. Usually, the moment I start talking about my brother, I had to fight hard to hold back the tears.

There was a faint trace of sadness in her voice and a flicker of sadness in her eyes, but that was it. She had come to term with it, but the fear was just under the surface, as I found out a couple of days back when the train came to a violent halt. In that instant, it's possible that she relived a nightmare she had suppressed since a long time.

"You cannot let the past rule you, and though it has been difficult and despite the fact that I miss them, everyone, I have accepted it and moved on with my life", Nicole said breaking my train of thoughts. She had a sad smile on her face which said more than any words could explain. I could see that she had almost let go of the past, but her parents were always in her heart and in her nightmares.

When someone close to you dies, it affects you deeply; a part of you dies with that person. The closer you are to the person, bigger that part. This happened when my younger brother was taken from us... That part will never come back or grow back. I am sure that when my parents leave this world, hopefully from old age, it will be the same with me.

It was almost like the words from that Aerosmith song... *There's a hole in my soul that's killing me forever.*

"A part of me died that day and left an emptiness that will never leave me, but like I said, I have learnt to live with it", she said, voicing my thoughts.

"I know how that feels. I had lost my younger brother in an accident. I had not accepted it for a long time, it was too difficult for me to accept it", I replied, surprisingly calm. Perhaps, the calmness she displayed had some effect on me as well.

"I am sorry for your loss Anand. Do you want to tell me what happened?" She asked me, leaning forward and meeting my eyes. I saw some sadness in her eyes, but she didn't really lose control.

I recounted very calmly, how I had lost my younger brother to a motorbike accident a few years back. I could see empathy in Nicole's eyes, and we felt closer to each other as we shared a similar experience of losing people we loved in similar situations. My own calmness as I talked to her surprised me.

The fact is that, in this world, there are people experiencing bigger pain than what I or Nicole was going through and I was fairly sure that I will probably never know such pain – People losing loved ones, people starving day in day out, people dying of diseases, people losing everything they owned to natural disasters. This was a very sobering realization for me. The fact is that people still deal with these situations without losing their maids or throwing a tantrum – the way I immaturely used to do. Reality is that they have learnt to live with it and be mature about it.

We didn't say anything for the next few minutes and were lost in the memories of loved ones that were violently taken away from us. We quietly sipped our drinks and I wondered what we should talk about next. Nicole was had nearly finished her drinks and she helped to make the decision for us.

"I am feeling quite tipsy now. I think I am done. Can we leave now, if you are okay?" she asked me, her words slurring a bit.

Although I was perfectly okay, and Nicole looked okay to me, it was clear that Nicole wanted to leave. I called for the bill and after much back and forth, the usual Chinese way, Nicole finally let me pay the bill. She thanked me for the dinner and to me, she looked happy with the fact that I paid the bill.

As we walked out of the restaurant, Nicole grabbed my arms and linked her arms with mine, making me blush visibly.

"Sorry, I am a bit drunk, and I don't want to trip and fall. I hope you don't mind", Nicole mumbled when she saw that I was blushing.

"No, no... It's fine", I said swallowing the lump my throat and trying to act natural. I could smell her perfume and it sort of personified her nature – positive and down to earth. It was a pleasant feeling... nothing sexual, but sort of relaxing, calming sense.

I walked with her to the place where she had parked her bike, but I was concerned that she might not really be able to bike back home, as she was starting to look drunk. I thought it would be better to take a taxi back home rather than risk biking all the way back in this state. The bike was double locked, and maybe we can move the bike near the hotel next to 96 Plaza, as that place is always well lit.

"Nicole, are you sure you can ride back home?" I asked her as we reached the parking lot, and added pointing at the hotel, "Let's take a taxi back home. We can leave the bike at that hotel and come back tomorrow."

"I am fine, I just need to get some fresh air", she replied confidently, unlinking her arms from mine and fishing out her bike key, but her words were slurring a bit.

"Okay, in which case, we will ride slowly and we will ride together", I offered as a compromise.

She smiled and nodded in agreement and that was that.

I spend the next couple of minutes, trying to find a Mobike with an adjustable seat. I was tempted to download Ofo app as most of them had adjustable seats, and it was good Mandarin practice for me. I finally found one about fifty meters away from where Nicole had parked her bike and unlocked it using my Mobike app.

We rode back very slowly and I relied on my phone to give me directions back home. The phone's voice-over directions were useless as the level of my Mandarin nosedives after a couple of drinks, so I relied solely on the arrow on the map to lead us back home. Nicole was humming some song and had a happy smile playing on her lips. Her bike was scarily wobbly, but given the amount of alcohol she had consumed, her balance was very impressive.

All the way, my attention was split between Nicole and my phone screen. I had a couple of scares as Nicole nearly lost her balance or when I nearly dropped my phone when I tried to maintain my balance and hold the handlebar with nothing but my left little finger.

We reached her community and I parked the Mobike outside community, in the designated bike parking area, while Nicole got off the bike and waited for me to lock the bike. I locked the bike and walked with her into the community. She seemed to have sobered up a bit, thanks to the bike ride.

I walked her to her apartment building. We didn't speak to each other and I guess there was no need to talk. We live in societies where your ability to "communicate" is confused with the ability to "speak" non-stop. She was happy and I was feeling more or less upbeat. We reached the apartment building and I knew I had to say something before I headed back home.

"Nicole, I had a great time today evening. I hope we can do this again some other time", I said bidding her farewell. I am not sure why, but I extended my hand awkwardly for a handshake.

She giggled at my awkward gesture and said, "Come on Anand... Don't be a stranger, give me a hug!"

I was surprised by this response and stood there awkwardly not sure if I should make the first move. Nicole sensed my hesitation, stepped close to me and hugged me. After a moment of hesitation, I hugged her back and started counting Mississippi's in my head. We let go of each other after three Mississippi's. We stood there for a moment smiling at each other.

"I had a great time too", Nicole said breaking the silence, "I too hope that we can meet some other time."

"See you around Nicole", I said barely able to stop smiling.

"See you around Anand", she replied.

I waited for her to get into the apartment building. Nicole swiped into the building and she turned around to wave a goodbye. I waved back and started walking back to my apartment. I was back home in my apartment complex in less than ten minutes. I got on to the lift and remembered that I have not seen my cell phone for a long time now and I might have messages from Jade. I took out the phone, unlocked it, and opened WeChat.

As I got into the apartment, I saw that there were some random messages from certain groups (messages in Chinese) and a couple of messages from Allen Huang, but there were no messages from Jade. I didn't think much of it earlier as I wanted to give her some space. I checked her moments and didn't see anything for the whole day, but then she had personal affair to complete so perhaps she was busy with that.

In any case, I decided that I should text Jade to see if she was doing okay.

```
Anand Nair (WeChat): Hey Jade.
Darling, I hope you are okay and hope
you are having a good time there. Do
text when you have time. I miss you.
```

I sighed and locked my phone and hooked it up to the charger.

I headed to the bathroom and took a quick shower. I towelled myself dry, dressed up for the night. I got into my bed and checked my phone for a response from Jade, but there were none. I sighed again, turned off the lights and got under the comforter. I was out in less than five minutes. As I drifted off into a peaceful slumber, I hoped that I would have some response from Jade in the morning.

I really could not wait for Jade to be back in Shanghai, and hold her in my arms.

Chapter 24.   Different Stages of Heartbreak

There were no messages from Jade the next day or the day after or the day after that. There would never be any more messages from Jade. Even though I was on the edge, and a bit angry, I resisted the urge to send nasty messages or try calling her.

Space is important, I told myself and I did not want to seem desperate; *Man up, don't let her control you* I reminded myself again and again.

As men, we all know we have to suppress our emotions and hide our true feeling from the world. This is one of the joys of being a man – the moment you show your emotions, you are seen as a weak sissy, who will not be respected by peers. It was also possible that the estate matters kept her occupied, though even I knew that was ridiculous – how long does it take to tap out a simple message like "I am okay" or "I miss you"? Not that long, really. I tried it out and it takes less than 10 seconds, even without auto-complete.

By the fourth day, fear and self-doubt replaced the anger. In my imagination, she was possibly seduced by an Italian or European playboy who was a million times more attractive than I ever could be, who as million times as smarter and she had more or less forgotten about me. I spend the next four days, messaging her on WeChat, and Facebook messenger, since it was possible that she might have lost her phone and she was not able to message me, so I wanted to cover all the possible avenues.

By the seventh day, I was sure she was intentionally ignoring my messages. I had also run out of patience and started calling her on WeChat and Facebook messenger hoping that this would somehow help... I was also confused as to why she hadn't just blocked me and put me out of my misery. If this was some sort of a sick power play, it was working. The tone of my messages went from normal to pleading to imploring to downright begging, with many "please" and "sorry" in most of the messages.

The eighth day, I was back at work, but work really had taken the back burner and I was barely able to keep away from my phone. Every time the phone vibrated, I thought it would be a message from Jade – which it wasn't – and would check my phone immediately, no matter what I was doing at that time or whom I was with at that time. Given my previous record, most of the people turned a blind eye towards my behavioural digression, which they thought might be temporary.

During this phase, I was fearful, angry and sad all the time.

I wanted closure, but it appeared that I was not going to get a closure from Jade Lin. In my imagination, she had played with me and used me to get to some ulterior goal – some other guy – by making him jealous of our "relationship". In my imagination, after she got the guy, she just ghosted me.

What can I say; the downward spiral was quick, nasty and thoroughly unimaginative.

The next stage was madness. I trusted my gut and my instincts so much that, I had convinced myself that she had found someone else, even though, there was no proof of this from the emotions Jade showed during the time we spent together or anywhere on the social media where I stalked her to find the reason she ghosted me.

Finally, I felt disgusted with myself, the way I desperately chased someone who clearly didn't want to be me.

For me, the conclusion of these insane thoughts was that, if she can so easily find someone else for no real apparent reason, I should do the same. My feelings for Jade, the infatuation I felt, the inability to let go, my personal insecurity all came gushing forth that instant.

The truth is that I never took a minute to look at this logically and calmly, but then logic and calm were all out of the equation at that point. After all, any logical man would have made efforts to ensure that the person he cares for is okay.

On the thirteenth day, the day before Allen Huang's party, I deleted the chat with Jade Lin and that evening, I went to one of the many clubs in Shanghai to celebrate my "freedom". After four hours of drinking and dancing (which was basically flailing my body around and occasionally throwing my hands up – I was never a good dancer, I will never be one), I started hitting on women there without any actual thoughts of next steps. If they turned out to be hookers, I moved on to the next target. On a scale of one to five, I was "absolutely hopeless" when it came to hitting on women. Despite this, I was my usual unrestrained drunk confident self that evening.

Even the question "Where are you from?" which usually meant the death of conversation after they get to know I am from India, didn't upset me. I used various responses like "Isn't it obvious that I am from India?" or "I am from land of Kamasutra" or "I will give you a clue – Slumdog Millionaire" or "I am not from the US, the UK, Europe, or Australia, as you can see from my accent" or even a bold "Does it really matter? It's not like we are going to get married anyway".

The last response was to as Eastern European or Russian lady who looked older than me. She was an average looking person, average height, but shorter than me and most of the other men in the club were ignoring her and she was busy ignoring some desperate club goers. I had walked up to her, introduced myself and asked her politely if I can join her for a drink. She was a bit surprised, possibly by my politeness, and nodded her head in agreement.

She introduced herself as Anastasia from Moscow who has been living in China for past fifteen years. She spoke jaw-dropping-good Chinese, at least when she ordered her booze.

We eventually started talking and soon started discussing our respective life in China. I was bullshitting about philosophy of life using a fake British accent, and had paused to take a drink, when she finally asked the question (Imagine this in Russian accent – "Where you from, Anand?") and I gave that answer, the one about getting married – and added in my normal accent, "... but, I am from India". She looked stunned for a moment before she burst out into a laughter. I knew that moment, that I had scored because I was expecting a slap.

We continued talking, but there was this perceptible expectation hanging in the air between us. We knew where this night was heading, but neither had a polite way to rush this forward. But thankfully, Ed Sheeran saved the day for us, with a remixed version of "Shape of You" which was what the DJ decided to play that moment. We took one look at each other, drained our drinks and hit the dance floor, where I gyrated wildly and she danced like an angel.

When the song was done we stepped out laughing and giggling and got the next round of drinks. I was not sure of the next move, and Anastasia sensed my hesitation. She leaned in and kissed me full on my lips, and it was surprisingly full of promises. The kiss was long and deep. When we finally broke the kiss, we knew the time had come for us to leave.

We finished our drinks quickly and headed to a nearby Motel 168. We both knew that this is not something we wanted to do in our apartment but in a neutral zone. The clerk knew exactly what we wanted and proactively offered us the 6-hour package in one of the better rooms.

We took him up on the offer.

When we parted ways during the wee hours of the next day, we didn't exchange our numbers but added each other on WeChat. With that, the silent agreement was in place – Anastasia Last-Name-Unknown (her WeChat also said just Anastasia) and I were unofficially friends-with-benefit and nothing else until one of us moves on in life. I was fairly certain it wouldn't be me. Also, I was not sure if there would be the next time, as these are one-shot deals.

I slept through the day and woke up at 3 PM. I checked my phone out of habit and there were a couple of messages, one from Allen and one from Anastasia. Obviously, I checked the message from Anastasia.

```
Anastasia (WeChat): Anand, it was fun
last night. Keep in touch.
```

The message from Allen was just a reminder for us to meet up for the party... Basically not really deserving a reply. I send him a thumbs-up in response. And sent a reply to Anastasia.

```
Anand Nair (WeChat): Anastasia, I had
fun too. Do keep in touch.
```

After a minute of thought, added.

```
Anand Nair (WeChat): PS: You want to
meet next weekend?
```

The response came five minutes later when I was in the toilet.

```
Anastasia (WeChat): Let us see. If
I'm free I will let you know.
```

I send a thumbs-up and a smiley in response.

That evening, I went to Allen's house for the party and this brought me face to face with Alice Wang, who claimed to be embarrassed with her behaviour the other day and proceeded to apologise for whatever she said. She claimed to be drunk at the time and was going through a bad phase.

Although I didn't buy that story, I told her it was okay, but she was clearly feeling very bad about her actions and wouldn't stop apologising. After three rounds of apology, I proposed we have a drink together to show that there were no hard feelings.

That one drink lead to a second and finally, I ended up spending the whole evening drinking and talking with Alice. Despite the fact that she was a bit of a racist, she was smart and funny… In the beginning.

After the third drink, she started rambling, in Chinese, about her past relationships including some Indian guy who dumped her like used up tea leaves when he was done with his China assignment. This sort of explained her anger towards Indians; this was personal rather than anything to do with racism. Also, despite her sweet innocent looks, she had some experience with men. What I understood from her, was that she was on a quest for true, eternal love. A quest that started soon after she discovered the love of her life – a rich Shanghainese, mama's boy – was cheating on her, with other men. He apparently wanted to experience how being with other men felt like.

To put it short, she clearly had bad luck when it came to relationships. Any other time, I would have felt some semblance of sympathy, but at that point, I was only thinking of how to get her into bed – she anyway hated Indians, there is not much I can do to make it worse… Well… maybe a little bit worse.

I pretended to listen to her woes and even showed some amount of sympathy. I even told her about my annulled marriage and how my ex-wife had ripped my life apart. I made it sound worse than what it was and made it sound like it happened yesterday. She was listening to me in rapt attention and by the end of the story, I could see that she was moved by my story, as she was touching my hands to show her sympathy and proposed another drink. She got further drunk and by the end of the evening she was nicely toasted, not that I was not drunk, but as we all know its relative – she was way more inebriated than me. When the time came to leave the party, I offered to drop her home as she also lived in Pudong, about four kilometres from where I was living.

In the cab, we talked some more about our love failures and regrets, before falling silent. She sighed loudly and leaned against my shoulder. As I turned to look at her, I could see she was looking at me and there was something in her eyes which screamed, "Do it". She slowly licked her lower lips and snuggled closer to me. There was a lump the size of a fist in my throat and I gulped it down silently. Her perfumes and her presence were driving me nuts. To say that I was sexually aroused would be putting it mildly, as my manhood was ready to rip a hole in my jeans.

I am not sure how but, after a couple of minutes or maybe a couple of seconds, we were kissing each other passionately. I slipped my hands under her blouse and caressed her lower back. She didn't resist and I let my hands roam over her body until I have my hands were on her breasts which were well-shaped and firm. She didn't resist that as well, so I let my hand drop gently until it dipped tentatively under the waist belt of her jeans. She abruptly broke the kiss and stared at me. I thought I had crossed some line as I couldn't read the expression in her eyes. She gripped my hand and instead of removing it, pushed my hand deeper into her panties. When I touched her centre, she moaned loudly and pressed closer to me. We kissed deeply with tongues duelling each other for real estate. We didn't really care about the taxi driver; in Shanghai, he should be used to this behaviour by now.

To me, it was apparent that I had a window of opportunity here to sleep with Alice. The only thought in my drunk brain was – *I want to fuck your brains out* – this thought was driven by my anger towards Jade's rejection, plain and simple. But... I was in a dilemma – I didn't want to do it only to have her complain later that I raped her after getting her drunk. As an Indian, whenever it comes to women, I live in perpetual and irrational fear of women claiming that I raped them after we slept together – I just didn't want to get caught in the media stereotypes about Indians being rapists especially since I don't know what they are writing about in China.

All those cautious thoughts evaporated when Alice started mumbling, "Take me home, Anand... Take me home and fuck me, Anand".

I managed an "Okay", in response before we continued with kissing and groping each other.

I didn't clarify if it is my home or her home, because we were anyways going to her home and I was sure as hell not going to take her to my apartment. Who was I to resist a beautiful woman who wants to sleep with me? Plus, it's not every day that I get an opportunity like this, given my average looks. You may call me selfish, but I know I am being realistic.

We soon reached her apartment complex and barely made it into her apartment. We stripped in the living room while kissing each other. She had a really nice, supple body, and I was thankful now that she had gone on her rant the other day so that this happened. I was so aroused that my boxers were strained to its limit. She saw this and nearly ripped off my underwear. She pushed me on to the couch and took me in her mouth. Even in my drunk state, it took all my willpower to not orgasm right there. The way she looked at me was not helping.

After about five minutes, she mumbled that we wanted me in her and tried to straddle me on the couch. Alice was so aroused that, she wanted to have sex without a condom. I sensible enough to fight her off for a few seconds to slip on a condom before she overpowered me and straddled me. She was really aroused and really uncontrollable. It was loud and crazy, with Alice screaming and moaning all the while. If I had some sense in me, I would have worried about the neighbours, but that moment was long gone.

She might have her personality issues but she was at the top of her form and very agile. We did it about five times before she started feeling tired. I was also exhausted by then. We lay together, panting and trying to catch her breath.

I excused myself to go to the bathroom and got out of the couch to go the bathroom and picked up the used condoms which were strewn next to the couch. I trashed the used condoms in the bathroom trash and relieved my bladder. It was almost as satisfying as the orgasms.

When I returned to the living room, I could see that Alice had curled up on the couch and passed out. I stood there for a few minutes to ensure that she was indeed asleep. She was still naked and was shivering a bit, as the living room was chilly. I went into her bedroom, found a comforter and covered her up, as I couldn't find the remote to her air conditioner. I didn't want to be seen as caring and all that, but I couldn't really be seen as that selfish as well. She sighed and curled further into the comforter. She had a smile on her face.

I dressed up quietly and left the apartment. I didn't want to be there when she woke up. In such scenarios, I knew my place – being not there when the girl wakes up for awkward exchanges that neither of us was looking forward to.

I stepped out of the apartment and on my way back home, I checked my phone out of habit to see if I had some message. There were no messages from Jade, two messages from Allen and some group messages, which I cleared out.

```
Allen Huang (WeChat): Dude, you left
with Alice?! I was hoping to catch up
with you.
```

The next message almost looked like an afterthought.

```
Allen Huang (WeChat): Dude, hope you
are not planning to hook up with
Alice. She can get a little crazy. I
would suggest being a bit careful.
```

Too late for that now, I thought, which was exactly my reply.

```
Anand Nair (WeChat): Dude, too late
for that now. The deed is done.
```

Allen must have been up cleaning up the house or finishing off the rest of the alcohol because he responded immediately.

> Allen Huang (WeChat): Oh, where did you do it? Your place, her place or Motel 168.

I was walking back home and I had reached an intersection where the walk signal was red.

> Anand Nair (WeChat): Her place. Five times.

The signal turned green and I crossed the road while avoiding a drunk electric scooter driver who was coming the other way.

> Allen Huang (WeChat): Okay. Word of advice - if there is a next time, don't take her to your house. Good night bro! Got to go now, Jean needs me.

I was looking at the map on my phone to figure out where to go next when that message came.

> Anand Nair (WeChat): No way she's coming to my place, I barely know her. Good night bro.

By then, I was sure what happened between me and Alice was a one-off thing. She would wake up, would remember what happened and would try to forget that the night ever happened. With that happy thought bouncing around in my head I light up a cigarette and increased the pace of my walk.

Turns out, the thing between me and Alice was not really a one-off thing. The chemistry we shared was so strong that we couldn't really stay away from each other. We met almost every other day at her place despite me telling her that I don't want anything exclusive with her. I told her about Anastasia, in hopes of upsetting her, but she had only one demand that whenever I am with Anastasia, I should also use condoms. She said that she wanted nothing more than to spend time with me, which basically meant a lot of fantastic sex in her house followed by lunch or dinner and then... more sex.

While I can genuinely say that I felt some amount affection for Jade, with Alice I felt nothing but an animalistic lust that translated to fantastic sex. The way she performed the act every time was an indication that she liked the sex as much as I did. To paraphrase Forrest Gump, 'the only way we didn't do it, is apart'.

At the same time, I met Anastasia once every week for dinner, drinks and a romp. We always used condoms and always kept it professional. We took turns in paying for dinner and motel, we never held each other's hands or left together from the motel or we never texted each other socially. Anastasia would quietly disappear from my life four weeks after we met. She had moved on with her life (she met someone on Tinder or OkCupid or something and wanted to make the effort) and we agreed to delete each other from WeChat, which by the way, we never did. I kept seeing her WeChat moments on a regular basis which meant that she didn't really delete me on WeChat.

Around the same time that Anastasia 'Doe' moved out of my life, stuff had started getting really weird with Alice.

She was getting upset with the fact that I had never shown her my apartment (I still went to her place to meet her). She was getting upset as I had not asked her for a date. She was getting upset that we were still using condoms (She was in an exclusive relationship with me, she claimed). She was getting upset that I was in an open relationship (I didn't tell about Anastasia moving on). She was getting upset for me not cuddling after sex (She felt used). She was getting upset that I was living in a rented apartment when I could stay in one of her apartments for free (Her family owned many). She was getting upset with the fact that I am taking the metro everywhere I go when I can take her spare car which had a Shanghai licence plate (A Smart-for-two). In short, she was getting out of control. But, when you are thinking with your genitals, you just don't know when to back off, until it is very late. That moment came around six weeks after our first encounter.

We were at her home, and she was on top, gyrating wildly and on the verge of orgasming. Her eyes were closed, and her back was arched as her orgasm built up in her. I was losing patience, so I thrust hard into her a couple of time and tipped her over the edge. She came, screaming "Oh my god! Anand... Honey, I love you!"

In retrospect, I wish I had left that instant, but that's not how these things work. Her orgasm triggered a massive orgasm in me, which in turn excited her into another orgasm. She collapsed on top me and started kissing me all over my face, moaning, and whispering, over and over "Oh baby, I love you".

I said nothing as I felt nothing. I didn't feel anger or panic or fear or sadness, but a certain numbness. I knew I had to end it. I don't want to deal with permanent commitments at this point. The only question was, how can I end it and when should I end it?

Also... Since I am soon going to be on a sex free diet, I might as well get some more of it when the going is good. It would just be like having that one all you can eat meat buffet before you go on a strictly vegetarian diet. With that happy thought, I removed the condom and slipped on a new one as soon as I was ready.

By the time I left that night, I had made her come seven times and she had made me come four times. I even cuddled her in between, which made her happier than all the sex we had till now. She went on proclaiming her love for me every time one of us orgasmed. At the end of it, she wanted me to stay with her through the night as she had assumed, incorrectly, all that sex meant I was in love with her too.

The reality was, I felt suffocated by her presence and I had to get out of there, but I was satisfied that I didn't end it without getting something out of this. I made some excuse about meeting my MBA friends the next day for brunch, as I got ready to leave her apartment. She fake-pouted for five minutes and then drifted off to sleep. This time I didn't bother to cover her with a quilt or anything.

On the way back home, I turned off the notifications for her phone number, her WeChat and left her a short message as I reached my home or "rented apartment" as she put it some time back.

```
Anand Nair (WeChat): Alice, sorry I
can't do this anymore. I can't be
with you, I am not capable of love.
You deserve better than me, I can't
give you what you want.
```

I wish I could say that I felt some guilt, instead, I felt nothing… Absolutely nothing… I slept like a baby that night.

Chapter 25.   Insanity Comes Calling

The next day, I talked to Allen and explained the situation to him. He obviously talked to Jean because, in less than twenty minutes, I got a few angry messages from her for me being an idiot and sleeping with Alice and after that, taking it so far.

Apparently, Alice has been crying and bawling non-stop as I was not answering her calls or was not responding to her messages on WeChat or iMessage. I have indeed been ignoring her calls (which was easy given that the notification for her calls was turned off) and I deleted her messages as soon as it arrived. I didn't want to really hear about how much she loves me and all that nonsense. She had been pressing Jean and Allen to disclose my address to her so that she could meet me and explain herself. Thankfully, they didn't want to get involved in this anymore and told her that they don't know where I lived.

Alice will be upset for a few days, maybe few weeks and then probably get back to her normal self, and yes... she probably will never date another Indian in her life again. I wish I could say that I feel bad about it, but not really. She just got caught in the crossfire. For me, Alice was a closed chapter, despite whatever thoughts she might have had about our "relationship".

The emotions that affected my mind and my actions were still seething in me. Despite the rebound sex, which I thought was the cure for heartbreak, all the anger, insecurity, fear and sadness were building up in me. I wanted closure, one way or another, but I couldn't find it. I assumed that more sex was the way to go forward... A part of me recognized, what I was doing is not in line with my basic personality and thus was "wrong". I knew that I was burning a lot of bridges, but I was not thinking straight at that point. It was entirely possible that Alice's family was well connected and they can destroy my life in China, but as I said before, I thought I was beyond care. I was walking the fine line between sanity and insanity and what was appropriate and inappropriate for a foreigner in China.

One call would push me over the edge, triggering the final phase of my heartbreak… bottomless grief and insanity.

It was around half past two in the afternoon on a Monday morning when the call came. I was at work and was with my team discussing some of the roadblocks in our current project. I was already irritable as the week was off to a very bad start and there was no real indication that it was going to get any better. So, when the phone started ringing, I cursed out loud. Given the fact that the call came through, I knew that this had to be a repeat call since I had put my phone in 'Do Not Disturb' mode before I got into the discussion with my team. As I excused myself and stepped out of the discussion room, I glanced at the phone, and I saw it was an international call starting with a country code I didn't recognize. Despite my ignorance, my heart and my mind started racing and my head was running through the possibilities. My irritability came down a notch as thoughts about Jade started racing through my head.

Was it possible that the call came from Italy? Was Jade calling me to apologise for what she put me through? Or Was she calling to end it, once and for all, unambiguously, with no loose ends at all? Or, is it just some random advertising call?

The questions were plenty, and answers were none until I answered the call to see who was on the other side. One part of me had started convinced myself that it was an advertising call, the other part was hopeful that it was Jade and she wanted to come back to me. I was more than willing to forget whatever that had happened, forgive her as long as she takes me back. I know, I am pathetic and shameless.

I slid the green button on my phone to the right and answered the call, "Hello?"

"Hello… Am I speaking to Anand?" the voice inquired politely. The voice on the other end was not that of Jade's, but that of an elderly woman who spoke with a heavy Chinese accent. The very first thing I heard in the voice was an immense sadness that was suppressed. This somehow felt familiar, but just couldn't place it. It was as if the person was holding back her tears. My instincts told me that I was not going to like what I was about to hear and my instincts told me that this call is about Jade.

"Hello? Are you there? Is this Anand? Anand Nair?" the voice repeated, snapping me back to reality.

"Er... Yes, this is Anand Nair. May I know who is calling?" I inquired after clearing my throat. I might be heartbroken, and going insane, but I had no reason to be rude to an elderly woman.

"Uhh... I am calling from Palermo in Italy. Umm... I am Jade Lin's mother..." She got to this point and before I could say anything in response, started sobbing uncontrollably. I knew immediately, that something was horribly wrong, that I have been horribly wrong about Jade and I have been a terrible human being in general.

Over the next few minutes, Jade's mother explained through the sobs, that Jade was in a car accident about two months back (the day after they reached Italy) and she had suffered severe brain trauma and multiple internal lacerations. According to the eyewitness reports, and dashboard camera recordings, Jade's car had drifted on to the oncoming lane, had swerved at the last second to avoid an oncoming semi-truck and crashed into a roadside tree. The car she was driving was totally smashed and the rescuers had to cut away a part of the car to get her out.

The head trauma and internal bleeding were so severe that, she had to undergo ten hours of surgery, and was kept on artificially induced coma post-surgery to avoid seizures. Despite the best efforts by the doctor there was no way she could be brought out of the coma, but she was kept on the ventilator as there was still some brain activity. About a week back she had woken up briefly, said the words "Anand... wait..." smiled at her mother, and slipped back into a coma.

Three days back, whatever brain activity monitors were registering, had ceased and Jade had slipped into a vegetative state. On the day before Jade's mother's call, the doctors and the family made the decision to pull her out of life support as there was nothing more that could be done. Since my name was the only thing that Jade spoke when she came to, and since my number was in her favourites, her mother had called to let me know what had happened, and that... Jade was not with us anymore.

I am not sure at what point I started crying but by the time Jade's mother had finished talking, I had tears flowing rolling down my cheeks. I ignored the concerned looks from my colleagues, as they walked by me; I am generally a cheerful guy and never had shown any negative emotions in the office. I was cold, light-headed and dizzy. There was a constant whining in my ear and the light in the room was getting dimmer.

Needless to say, the guilt was also building up in me by the second. It felt like someone had placed a huge rock on my chest and the lump in my throat just refused to budge. I had assumed the worst about Jade and I was cheating on her while she was literally dying.

Jade's mother was asking me something and when she repeated the question, I snapped out of my dazed state.

"How well did you know Jade?" she asked me again.

I tried to speak but no sound came out. I cleared my throat before trying to speak again. I was not sure what exactly to tell her, and after few seconds I decided to tell her what I felt was the best thing to say under the circumstances. The truth.

"Umm... We are... were seeing each other, madam... We were in a relationship", I said when I found my voice.

The line went silent for a minute, and I could hear Jade's mom's wavering breaths coming down the line. I knew that she was about to burst into tears again. I walked into an unoccupied conference room to avoid any more stares. The moment I entered the conference room, she started wailing again and this time it sounded almost animalistic. It was the most heart-wrenching sound that I had heard in my life. I didn't know what to do, or what to say, so I just kept quiet and waited. I will never know why she cried at this discovery, but selfishly, I hoped that it was not because of the fact that her daughter was seeing an Indian. After about couple minutes of crying uncontrollably, she mumbled something, of which I caught the word "Sorry", after which she disconnected the call.

I sat in the conference room for a very long time, staring at the phone, and waiting for something, but I was not sure what it was; I guess I was waiting for that pain in the chest to subside or Jade's mom to call back or me to stop crying. The pain in the chest wouldn't subside for days, Jade's mother would never call back and the tears wouldn't stop for next couple of hours. I wept silently in that tiny conference room until there were no tears left to shed. Finally, at around 5:00 in the evening, I sent a text message to my team members apologising for dropping the ball, quietly slipped out to the office while avoiding eyes of my colleagues who saw me crying and headed back to my home.

I spent that evening chain smoking and drinking heavily while looking at photos Jade and I had taken together. There was a lot of regret, guilt and anger, for being a selfish, inconsiderate human being and, for deleting Jade's WeChat messages. I finally could cry out loud and that's exactly what I did – I cried shamelessly and I wept for hours. A thought that really didn't help with my situation, one that had been nagging me since Jade's mother called me, was if my last text message to her actually distracted her and finally led to the accident. Logically, it was possible.

This was a very overwhelming and painful thought, as it meant that I was directly responsible for the death of someone I may have been in love with... No! A person I WAS in love with and a person I still loved. The loss made the love real; until that moment it was all about anger, doubts, fears and options, but when I lost Jade for good, that was when I knew what I felt for her was love. Now, it was not pure, unselfish love that one might read in books or see in movies, but it was real love, which was selfish, jealous and flawed like in real life. True love, just like real life, is not perfect. At that moment, I realized I would have given anything for Jade to be still alive, even if she was not with me.

This gnawing thought, that I might be responsible for her death, meant that, I couldn't sleep that night or the following night. Whenever I dozed off, I would have one of those nightmares of being in a car crash with Jade and the reason for the car crash would invariably be because I distracted her one way or another. I would usually wake up with my heart pounding in my chest, my torso covered in cold sweat and me on the floor. The worst part of this nightmare was not that I couldn't sleep afterwards, but it was the fact there was this metallic sweet smell of blood in my head that refused to go away and I could hear Jade's screams. I would spend rest of the night praying to any God willing to hear my prayers to wake me up from this long and horrible nightmare like the way I woke up from the previous nightmare. But, I knew the truth, this was no nightmare, this was happening.

In fact, I would sleep properly only after a week – a week that I spent barely keeping up with work, drinking large amounts of coffee by the day and larger amounts of alcohol by the night, neither eating anything nor sleeping well and trying to convince myself that I couldn't be responsible for Jade's death. By the time, I fell into a deep, fatigue and alcohol-induced sleep, the opposite had happened – I had convinced myself that I was responsible for Jade's death, even though there were a dozen possible explanations for the accident.

Two weeks after the call, I threw myself into my work to try to keep my mind sane, and to drown the voice in my head that repeated day and night, that I killed my Jade. I ended up was working sixteen to seventeen hours a day. I slept less than five hours a day and developed dark circles that made me look like the demon. I had also started losing weight as I was not getting enough food – most of my calories coming from instant noodles or instant pasta, black coffee and alcohol. I had stopped shaving and cutting my hair and I was starting to look more and more like unkempt as the days passed. I was smoking close to two packets of cigarettes daily and my stamina was getting destroyed, really fast. I had stopped talking to most of my friends and my extended family, with official conversations kept to the barest minimum possible and at a professional level so that I don't blurt out something absurd in a moment of grief.

People in office started noticing the abrupt change in me as I was generally a cheerful character who like talking and joking around with my colleagues and used to constantly invite colleagues for lunches, coffee or drinks. Some folks who were closer to me politely inquired what was wrong for which my response was "personal issues" with no further explanation. I declined their offers to go out for lunch or coffee and claimed to be busy. After a while, they stopped inquiring about my well-being and stopped inviting me out, which suited me just fine. To ensure that there were no more questions, what I did do was to use a lot of gel to get my wild hair under control.

My only tenuous link to sanity were my parents, my sister, and Allen & Jean. I made an effort to talk to them or meet them. I managed to be pleasant with them, but it took a lot of mental effort to maintain the façade, but I felt it was essential to maintain the act to ensure that they were not too worried. I explained the weight loss and appearance as a result of my busy work schedule, which was sort of true, but refused to elaborate further what was happening in my life. I stopped responding to text messages from most of my other friends and even declined invitations from Nicole Zhang for coffee or lunch. I couldn't get the thought out of my head that I was having a good time with Nicole when Jade was slowly dying. Eventually, Nicole stopped messaging, possibly had figured out that something was off and like for everyone else in my life, I dropped off her radar and she, from mine.

My sense of guilt was intense and I went deeper and deeper into a dark, suicidal depression, but had come to the decision that work, alcohol and cigarettes would help me manage my condition. The only thing that kept me from killing myself was the thought that my parents and my sister cannot stand another loss. I might be selfish, but not that selfish that I would put my parents, my sister or my dear friends through the same hell I was going through.

Given my excessive dependency on work, weekends and holidays turned out to be unbearable. Since a lot of my work depended on my team, there was no way I could work alone on weekend. I had no reason to get out of my bed, and I spent hours laying and staring at the ceiling and wishing that time would pass faster. I would sometimes, bury my head in the pillow and scream hard until I had no voice left. On weekends, I often whipped myself using my leather belt, just so that I can divert the attention using pain.

I had lost interest in outdoor activities. I used to previously enjoy biking or hiking, which was something that helped me when I felt troubled. The only thing that kept me from going totally insane and ensured that I pass time faster, was long meandering walks around the city trying to find some meaning for my existence. Obviously, I avoided going to places like the bund where Jade and I had spent time together. Sometimes, a familiar sight would trigger some memory with Jade and that would reduce me to tears – I wanted to avoid emotional outbreaks in the public.

I wanted to leave Shanghai for good but was mentally incapable of looking for a new job. Nor was I in any sort of financial situation where I could take a long break – which basically meant I was stuck in Shanghai. I could leave the job and go back to India, but that would bring more scrutiny from my parents and relatives. That… I was in no position to handle.

My walk around the city, usually ended up with me going to my usual watering hole, where I would ignore everything and everyone else but my drink. I would drink whiskey or vodka until the wee hours of the morning, hoping that it would ease the pain in me. I would stumble out of the bar at two or three in the morning and hail a ride back home. I would barely make it home before passing out on my couch or bed.

A bit about this place I go any further... Here we had a sort of unwritten agreement that we let each other be. This is not a place you come to hangout with your friends nor was this a place where you come to meet new people. This is a place where we come to escape from whatever we were running from, have a couple of solitary drink or ten and enjoy some quiet time. And, as a foreigner, I even had the privilege of just pointing at what I wanted on the menu and get what I wanted without even uttering a single word.

This is the reason why I kept coming back here – The owners, the staff and patrons were very professional in the sense that we valued each other's drunken space. I loved the anonymity this place gave me and loved the fact that no one gave a fuck. We were all silent drinkers and the most amount of communication that happened in our little world was when bartender nodded his head at the regular dipsomaniacs.

There was no better way to put this – I was hiding from the world, hiding from my friends and family, and hiding from myself. Meanwhile, I was trying to hurt myself as much as possible in the process. I drank like a fish, smoked like a train engine and got by with barely enough sleep or food. I was not getting enough exercise nor was I interested in doing anything outside my area of comfort. I didn't want to shave or get a haircut, as those meant, I need to have unnecessary conversations. I stopped my Chinese lessons as that required some amount of motivation to stay in China, which I lacked at that point.

People in the office tried to understand, my new-found obsession with work, but I guess after a point, the bosses were happy that I was doing two people's work for about 80% of one person's wage (I was a bad negotiator). This, of course, pissed off some of the people in office who worked normal 8-hour days. Some people even complained to the HR that I was a disturbing influence to the others, but after a quick review with the managers, it was decided as long as I don't listen to Indian music in office while working, I can continue working the way I was working. The normal me would have been offended, but then the normal me would have been more normal and wouldn't have really pissed off my colleagues, even when I had disagreements with them.

Usually, I would travel to India couple of times a year, once during the Chinese New Year and once during the National Holidays, which sort of helped to give me a culinary and cultural break. This year, I was not capable of facing my parents, friends or anyone else, so I made some excuse for heavy workload to avoid going to India.

The heavy smoking & drinking, lack of proper nutrition and lack of rest would all lead to aggravation of my mild asthma to full-blown pneumonia, which I didn't get treated until I reached a point where I was coughing uncontrollably and spitting blood all the time.

I finally went to the hospital when I developed a fever so bad that, I could barely walk from my bed to my bathroom. Despite repeated requests and warnings by my doctor over my multiple visits, I refused to get admitted to hospital for proper treatment or even reduce my smoking. I compensated for my smoking with strong antibiotics and asthma inhalers, which further weakened me. My doctor could clearly see that I was depressed and advised me to talk to a psychiatrist. This advice predictably fell on deaf ears and I withdrew deeper into a dark corner within my sub-conscious, while my life continued on auto-pilot.

This downward spiral would continue unchecked for four months until that day at Starbucks. The day I would pass out due to hunger & fatigue; the day Nicole would fail to recognise me; the day I had my moment of clarity.

Chapter 26.   Carpe Diem

At times, those seemingly life-changing events, aren't life-changing and seemingly insignificant events turn out to be life-changing. Whatever it may be, logic, reason and root cause behind these events cannot be understood (at that point) and as one matures, and as time passes, the answer might come to light. It will be like finding that long-missing piece of the puzzle.

The "Eureka!" moment...

Meanwhile, the only thing that you can do is to be true to yourself and be ready to accept that your intuition might be wrong. Equally important is the fact that, some of these questions may never be answered. That is okay, it just means one has to learn how to let go of things for which there are no answers.

This is the reality of life.

By the time I reached back home from the Starbucks on the bund, I accepted that I am possibly never going to know what happened on that day and how Jade got into that accident. There was no point in trying to beat myself over things from the past I cannot change. No amount of alcohol or cigarettes would change the fact that Jade is gone forever and, maybe its time for me to move on with my life. I needed a way to move forward, and I needed a way to cope with the pain.

But before I go any further I needed to clean up my act. I started by throwing out all the alcohol at my home. After I had thrown out the last bottle of alcohol, I headed to my bathroom, and took a long hot shower, not because I was feeling dirty, but to soften my beard. After about ten minutes under the hot shower, I stepped out of the shower and towelled myself dry. I disconnected my electric shears which had been charging since I came back home. I set shears to zero and started trimming my moustache and beard over the wash basin. It took me nearly fifteen minutes to carefully trim down my facial hair to an even short stubble. I was startled by the reappearance of a once familiar face, but a bit leaner and a lot paler than what it used to be six months back. I finished by trimming the sideburns.

I used a wet napkin to clean out the hair from the wash basin. I lathered up shaving foam on my face, put a new blade into my razor and carefully started shaving. Now that I looked a bit more human, I decided that I needed a haircut. I got dressed up and took a Mobike to a nearby salon run by a gay couple. I used to be their regular customer and they were happy to see me back. From my appearance, they guessed correctly that they didn't lose me as a customer, but had stopped cutting my hair, for whatever reason. I got my usual haircut done and I looked almost normal.

I decided to walk back home and despite having to walk past at least five shops that sell cigarettes, I managed to reach back without falling off the wagon. I know it has been only a couple of hours or so since I quit smoking, but I was proud of myself, as the first few hours were crucial for me to survive on the wagon.

I spend next couple of hours on Taobao buying, browsing for nicotine gums and vape machines. After I selected the product that seemed promising, I headed out to Century Park for a walk as my mind was starting to wander towards tobacco and alcohol. My brain was already starting to rationalize and pushing me to get that nicotine or alcohol high, and it was only half past four in the evening. My brain was trying to convince me that it is okay to smoke a light cigarette or that I should celebrate quitting smoking by having a couple of beers or maybe a martini.

While those thoughts were not completely eliminated, walking 15 kilometres around the Century Park, certainly helped to quieten the noise in my head. It took me three hours, and I was exhausted, and breathless by the end.

As I walked around the park, I tried to push thoughts of Jade out of my mind, only to realize that more I try to stop thinking about Jade, the more I thought about her. Just as the pain of losing my brother was always there with me, the pain of losing Jade will always be there with me. I had to find a way to manage that pain rather than let that pain control me for the rest of my life. I don't mind it if the pain helps to shape my character, but I don't want it to shape my life.

I also knew that it's time for me to bring back the people I care for back into my life, beginning with my family and my close friends. I would speak about this, voice my pain to people who love me, rather than let it seethe in my soul. There might be tears and emotions, but I needed to get this weight off my mind.

I was ravenous by the time I reached home and ordered a large dinner of fried chicken curry, omelette rice, a large salad, and pan-fried meat dumpling from a Japanese curry house using one of the many delivery apps. I was not sure if I could finish the whole thing but decide to order extra just in case. As I waited for the delivery to come, I took another long hot shower.

After my dinner had arrived, I started exploring some comedy movies on Youku (Chinese Youtube), as I badly needed to laugh, and finally ended up selecting some animated movie series about a fat panda learning Kung-fu. I had seen the whole series before, but I was amused all the same and I surprisingly managed to complete my very large dinner, as I enjoyed the first part of the series.

I turned in early and slept deep. There were no more nightmares or dreams.

I woke up early the next day, feeling refreshed and resisted the urge to find a cigarette. I did some light callisthenics at home and went a walk around the Century Park. I walked as quickly as I could and let the walk clear my mind. By the end of the walk, I was sure of what I needed to do right away – I needed to share my grief with people who cared for me – my parents & my sister, Allen Huang & Jean Li, and perhaps, even Nicole.

As I took shower to get ready to meet Nicole, I realized a few things. I have learnt the hard way that bottling up the emotions, denying what you feel and being dishonest to yourself are the worst thing that can happen to you. It's even worse than losing someone you love – you lose yourself and your soul. The person you were will be destroyed and only an empty shell of the person you were will remain.

In retrospect... There are a lot of things that could have happened in retrospect, and in life there is no going back, only going forward, so I have to live the moment. But one thing is clear, if you love someone, or care for a person, make sure that the person knows it because you never know what life has to offer in the next moment. Later it might to too late to appreciate what you have.

If you wait for the time to be ready, and get it perfect and be sure, you might just be too late.

I had made up my mind to get back to my life and continue living in Shanghai, instead of running away from Shanghai. The pain I felt now, will eventually fade. The grief I felt, will eventually wane. Experiences and memories shape us. I wanted my memory of Jade and the time I spent with her, however brief, to define me as the person I will become in the future.

As I walked to the metro, I texted my parents and told them that I loved them and that I missed them, and I promised to travel to India as soon as I can to meet them. Just as I reached the metro, messaged my boss and explained to her that I need a month's vacation as soon as possible. Surprisingly, the response was positive, and she also added that I should take care of myself, which is more than what I deserved, given my recent behaviour.

When in the metro, I texted Allen and told him that I would like to meet up with him as soon as possible and talk to him about what has been happening in my life. He replied when I reached the Lujiazui station.

```
Allen Huang: Finally! Jean and I knew
there was something wrong with you
but didn't want to press you. You are
more welcome to come whenever you
want. You can stay with us for a few
days if it helps.
```

I replied immediately that I will visit them as soon as possible.

I swiped out of the metro and walked to Blue Frog. I was feeling a bit apprehensive as the Blue Frog that I was going to was right next to the TGI Friday's, where Jade and I had our dinner date. I steeled myself and walked faster towards the restaurant. I felt the phone go off in my hand and saw that Nicole had texted me. She had already reached Blue Frog and had got a table for us. She also gave me the table number. I thanked her and told her that I am about five minutes away.

As I entered Blue Frog, I saw the ever so beautiful Nicole Zhang sitting in the corner studying the menu. As if on cue, she looked up and saw me. She gave me her patented dazzling smile and waved at me. If my gaunt appearance shocked her, she didn't show it. She stood up to greet me and gave me a warm hug. It felt good and I hugged her back fiercely. I apologised profusely for not keeping in touch.

"It is fine, Anand, I understand", she said continuing to hug me.

I knew that moment, everything was going to be okay and I was going to be okay.

Life is never easy, and there might be dark moments, but when you have pillars like your family or friends like Allen or Jean or Nicole in my life, you will find the courage and strength you need to move forward.

EPILOUGE

Eighteen months had passed since that day at Starbucks and I was still on the wagon. I have not picked up a cigarette or drank alcohol since that day, and my friends and family had helped me get through that dark phase of my life. There were many more days of disappointments, but Allen, Jean and Nicole, along with my family stuck with me and ensured that I don't fall back into despair. It took months for the nightmares to stop haunting me, and I finally went to a psychologist to talk about stuff that was troubling me. This helped somewhat, but what really helped me was guided Zen meditation, that helped me calm my mind and live the moment.

Nicole and I picked up right where we left off, and I started meeting her more for helping her company with growth strategies, until the day she mustered up the courage to ask me if I would like to become a full-time partner in the company to help her with operations and innovation. This was about six months after the day at Starbucks and after the seed VC money had come through. As I knew a lot about the business by then and I had somewhat helped to negotiate the deal with the VC firm, she wanted to offer the job to me, before she considered anyone else. The salary she offered me was just enough to survive if I moved into a smaller apartment, but she also offered me 10% of the company as part of the deal. I accepted after considering the offer for the whole of sixty seconds, give or take a few seconds.

We are now preparing to raise Series A funding and the prospects of securing the funding from the same VC firm looked very promising. If this does work out, we plan to move to the headquarters to Xiamen and scale our operations out of Xiamen. I have volunteered myself to move to Xiamen and hoped to celebrate my next birthday in Xiamen. I was very positive that would happen.

Jade remains in my heart, but now she inspires me to be a better version of myself. Her demise reminded me that I should live a little bit more and do what I really want to do, rather than what others wanted me to do. I have accepted that I love Jade and will continue to do so for a very long time, but I was ready to move on.

Jade would have wanted that.

Made in the USA
San Bernardino, CA
12 June 2018